ECLIPSE OF THE JAGUAR

ECLIPSE OF THE JAGUAR

MacGregor Family
Adventure Series
Book Seven

a novel by

Richard Trout

PELICAN PUBLISHING COMPANY
GRETNA 2011

Library of Congress Cataloging-in-Publication Data

Trout, Richard.
Eclipse of the Jaguar : a novel / by Richard Trout.
p. cm. — (MacGregor family adventure series ; bk. 7)
Summary: While the MacGregor family is in Belize exploring Mayan temples, thirteen-year-old R.O. and his new friend, Katelynn, are kidnapped by looters.
ISBN 978-1-58980-872-0 (hardcover : alk. paper) [1. Adventure and adventurers—Fiction. 2. Archaeology—Fiction. 3. Mayas—Antiquities—Fiction. 4. Indians of Central America—Antiquities—Fiction. 5. Kidnapping—Fiction. 6. Ecology—Fiction. 7. Belize—Fiction.] I. Title.
PZ7.T7545Ecl 2011
[Fic]—dc22
2010054222

The entirety of this novel is a work of fiction and bears no resemblance to real people or events. The MacGregor teens perform daring deeds that should not be attempted by any minor without the advice and consent of an adult.

Printed in the United States of America
Published by Pelican Publishing Company, Inc.
1000 Burmaster Street, Gretna, Louisiana 70053

For Emma Kate, Noah Paul, and Micah Harrison
May your lives be rich and full of adventure!

Table of Contents

Acknowledgements

A special thanks to Dr. Neal Coates of Abilene Christian University, my resident political scientist and trusted associate; to Mr. Steve Jarman, my personal dive master and SCUBA advisor; and all the teachers who write to me, sharing stories about how their kids relate to ***The MacGregor Family Adventures***. Many thanks to Dr. Robert Lamb and Health Talents International for their continued heroism in providing medical aid to the people of Central America.

I would also like to thank all of the tireless and fearless scholars who explored the "land of the Maya" for their most excellent research, their personal sacrifices and daring, and the wonderful books they have written. I could spend a lifetime reading and never read them all. Great stories cannot be told without the men and women of many nations who spent decades discovering the mysteries of this ancient and amazing culture.

Crawling through these temples and passageways made my heart beat rapidly and chills run all over my skin from the excitement. To view the intricate murals firsthand was indeed a wonderful experience. Spending much time in the

Museum of Anthropology in Mexico City and the British Museum in London gave me an added appreciation of what has been preserved from the "forest of the kings." Even though I speak Spanish, I appreciate the museum staff for pointing out that the letter X is pronounced "sh" when reading Mayan words translated from their hieroglyphs. This note will help out all of you readers.

Also, a big thanks to David North for his ingenuity and talents in taking my novels to kids around the globe through the internet. With each novel I write, the list of people who contribute to my success grows and grows, and that includes hundreds of teachers and librarians who share my books with their students. And I would be totally remiss if I didn't thank Dr. Milburn Calhoun and all the wonderful people who make up the Pelican Publishing organization around the world.

—Richard Trout

Prologue

Calakmul, 695 A.D., Deep in the Heart of the Mayan World

The twelve-year-old boy struck the sides of the drum firmly. Sweat poured down his bare back. The warmth of the cavern with the roaring fire made it hard to breathe. The resonant hollows of the wooden drum, called a teponaztli, thrust mellow tones through the air as though they were arrows piercing the shroud of night. With each rhythmic blow, the wooden mallet struck the ancient ceremonial drum just behind the ornately carved heart of a sacred warrior of Ab Kim Xac, the god of war. There was a long procession of people who had walked slowly up the mountain trail. The flames from torches along the trail illuminated the treacherous path overlooking the cliff that reached down to the clear pool of water below. Even more torches lined the edges of the pool so it could be seen clearly.

When he had marched through the small opening of the hot cavern, the young boy had no idea that the cave was a giant underground water hole that was sacred to the Mayans. He robotically kept the rhythm with two other drummers while gazing around at the sites that were so different from his rainforest home.

When the sun stood high in the sky, the processional met at the valley's rim, where the light penetrated the clouds of steam and smoke from a nearby volcano. There were four young boys, twelve warriors, five servants, and two priests of Nagual attired as wild animals, each an animal of the gods with magical powers.

At the exact moment the priests turned toward the drummers, the beating stopped, and the priests began to chant. The Jaguar appeared. He was Jaguar Paw, the supreme ruler of Calakmul. His eyes, though marbled red and yellow with age, reflected the excitement of the moment. A man of strong stature, he stood regally at the foot of the ancient stone path overlooking the pool below. Torches had been thrown over the side, landing on the rocks alongside the pool and illuminating the great cavern.

Jaguar Paw's headdress reached above and behind him at least a foot. The green and yellow tail feathers of parrots accented the white feather of the toucan and macaw and the beautiful green of the quetzal bird. A headband of tanned iguana rested on his gray eyebrows, blending in with the pits and crevices of the aged leader's face. His mantle hung squarely from his shoulders and lightly touched the top of his gold sandals, which had gold leaf tassels and a solid gold footplate. As he turned and raised his arms, the white light of the straw torches illuminated the mantle draping from his shoulders. The mantle was nearly five-and-a-half-feet long, made of alternating strips of ocelot and jaguar skins. Bright, colored threads of dark red, purple, and blue held the skins in place, providing a beautiful patchwork display of skilled tailoring. The outside trim was a three-inch-wide snakeskin that was unbroken the entire length of two sides and the top. Down from ducks marked the joining of the ocelot and the snake.

The last person in line stood behind Jaguar Paw in a white tunic. Her light-brown skin dimpled when a cool breeze blew from the depths below. She was a goddess of beauty, about to be the bride of Kinich Ahau, the god of the sun. The processional stopped and the drums began to softly beat. The priest read from a scroll:

> "The precious god of the sun, who gives us life, goes through the chambers of evil when the darkness comes. We pledge our lives to this god and offer him companionship through this dark journey that he may have favor with us."

The priests took hold of the young woman and laid her upon the large altar next to the ledge overlooking the pool below. She quickly closed her eyes. She seemed to be in a trance. The priest began again:

> "We pray, oh Jaguar, that you will protect us from famine, from drought, from the fear of death.
>
> We pray, oh Tlaloc, that the tears of children who we have sent to you will fall upon our precious forest and make the seed of all things begin to grow.
>
> We pray that Hun Nal Ye will raise her maize from the earth to feed her children.
>
> We pray, oh Itzam Na, that our enemies will lie prostrate at our feet and the blood of our enemies will quench your thirst and nourish our souls.
>
> As warriors of the sun, and servants of the moon Ix Chel, we beseech the stars to allow your glory to rise again to warm the face of man."

The priest pointed toward the young boy with the drum, and two warriors immediately grabbed him. The drum hit the hard pathway and bounced over the ledge. A few seconds later, they heard the splash as it hit the pool below. The young boy never spoke, but he could guess what was happening. He had seen it before. When a sacrifice of great importance was given to the gods, a companion was chosen to go along the way. His legs fell limp and he couldn't walk. Fear surged through his body.

As he was dragged near the sacrificial stone where the

young woman lay ready to give her heart to the priest and then be thrown into the pool below, the boy felt something warm being splashed on his skin. He looked down and saw he was covered in blue oil. He had seen it before when slaves where painted blue and then their heads were chopped off, leaving their bodies to flail wildly and fall from the top of the sacred altar high atop the pyramid.

"Oh no," he said with all his strength, but it came out as a whisper.

"Oh no," he tried again. This time the young woman on the altar turned to look at him with a puzzled expression.

"This can't be! I am a good boy!" the young drummer yelled, his voice now loud and echoing through the cavern.

He was now completely covered in blue from head to toe. He could feel the coolness of the sacrificial stone pressed up against his back as a warrior stepped forward and raised an axe high in the air. He could feel someone pulling on his hair, stretching his neck. Then, suddenly, they all heard voices entering the cave.

Jaguar Paw looked up and then around. The warrior lowered the axe and the young woman sat up on the stone. The noise was near the entrance of the cave. It sounded like dozens of voices and it was getting louder.

"It is Jansaw Chan. He's come to take Calakmul," Jaguar Paw said firmly.

The warriors drew their weapons and ran toward the entrance with Jaguar Paw right behind them, ready to face their enemy and his warriors from Tikal. The priests retreated to the hidden crevices in the cavern.

The muscular and fit army of Tikal rushed into the cave, killing the first priests they encountered. The Calakmul warriors drew their swords and dove into the battle. The Tikal warriors were known for their blood-thirsty battle methods of killing all men, women, and children of conquered city-states. Their feathered headdresses and snake-skin belts made them appear like exotic gods sent to mete out justice to nonbelievers. They were, in fact, the oppressors of the Maya who sought out the wealth and productive forests of their enemies. The Calakmul warriors knew that if they lost, their families would die a horrible death.

The young boy looked over at the beautiful girl and then reached for her hand. She stepped down from the sacrificial altar and followed him to the ledge overlooking the pool.

"That is our only way to escape," he said.

"But I was meant to be a loving sacrifice to Itzam Na. I wanted that," she said.

"Maybe later," the young boy said and jumped over the side, pulling the screaming young woman behind him.

They hit the water feet first and the coolness of the pool felt good to both of them. The drummer boy began to try to wash some of the blue off of his skin.

"I can't swim," the young woman called.

"Don't worry, I can," the boy replied and started to pull her through the water toward the side of the pool that was still lit with the smoking torches.

The fighting had spilled into the cave. There was yelling and screaming as the armies of Calakmul and Tikal fought wildly. Occasionally a dead body would fall over the side of the cavern and the children would hear a splash. The two worked their way to the bank and crawled out on a thick ledge to hide and wait out the battle. It raged on for what seemed like hours.

When silence came, there was total darkness. The young woman and the boy shivered in the coolness of the pool until they could see light penetrating the thin tunnel leading into the cavern. The boy cautiously swam back across the pool, pulling the young woman behind him, and carefully climbed up to the rocky ledge until they could stand next to the sacrificial stone. The young woman touched it and then shuttered.

"I don't think I'm ready to die," she said.

"Nor I," the young boy replied.

Together they walked toward the small entrance to the cave, past fallen warriors, until daylight was shining on them through the canopy of the rainforest. Looking around for the battle, all they found were bodies of warriors, mostly from Calakmul. Tikal had scored a surprise attack. Walking slowly, they finally reached the ridge that looked down into Calakmul from the east. The city was in ruins, with people lying dead or tied to poles. They even saw heads scattered everywhere without bodies. Standing at the top of the sacred pyramid was Jaguar Paw. Facing him was the ruler of Tikal, Jansaw Chan K'awill I.

As the two youths looked on, they saw that the sky was darkening with clouds; it would soon be a storm. Though this commonly happened in their jungle, they felt a sense of dread, knowing that their city has just been devastated.

Jaguar Paw was made to kneel and suddenly a warrior stepped forward and chopped off his head. The Tikal warriors all around cheered and began to release all of the prisoners. Jansaw Chan knew they would fight no more.

"Look there, two more to sacrifice," said a voice from behind the children.

They turned to see several Tikal warriors running their way. Without exchanging a word, they ran to their right, following a path into the forest. The young boy held on to the girl's hand as he pushed large philodendron leaves out of the way and jumped over branches that had fallen from the trees above.

"When I let go, you must keep up with me or you will die today," he said as he released her hand.

"Yes, I understand," she replied, her head now clear of the drugs she had been given before the planned sacrifice.

The two raced through the forest like deer as the storm clouds broke and rain began to fall heavily, with raindrops splattering on the broad leaves of the forest foliage sounding like pebbles falling from the sky. But the vicious warriors, even though they were clad in armor and weapons, kept up with them. An arrow zipped past the youths as they turned onto another path. Then two more arrows broke branches over their heads, just above them. The girl cried out and the young boy reached back and grabbed her hand again.

"Don't say anything; they'll know our direction," he said to her as quietly as he could.

The young woman just nodded and stayed close behind him.

Seeing a turn in the jungle path ahead, the boy pointed in the opposite direction and the girl acknowledged his sign, nodding quickly. Her eyes were wild and her breathing was fast from keeping up with her racing heart and bare feet that pounded the pathway. By this time the rain had increased, almost to a downpour. When they reached the turn, the boy reached back and yanked with all of his might. Because she was taller than the boy, she tumbled forward on top of him as they left the trail and began sliding down a steep incline that the boy knew was the side of the mountain.

The boy had never been this way before and didn't know what lay ahead as they tumbled head over heal, further and further away from the trail above. Even with the cracking of small branches and their exhausted breathing, they still heard the warriors run by and stay on the trail that led toward the top of the mountain.

As the children stopped rolling and began to get their balance, the boy reached out and grabbed a low-hanging branch to slow his motion.

The young girl tried to stand up, but she began to sink into the muck of the trail.

"It's moving," she said loudly.

"What's moving?" the boy said and looked around.

"The trail. It's moving!" she exclaimed with a frightened look on her face.

"That's not possible," he responded quickly.

Suddenly, the muddy side of the mountain began to slide, brining them with it.

She reached out and grabbed the boy, and together they

fell into the muck of the forest as it slid downhill, gaining speed and taking more plants and fallen branches with them.

The girl screamed out as their momentum continued to build, until they had no control over destination or speed. Tree limbs and rocks battered them on the head and scratched their bodies. With each rock or piece of wood that hit them, the children would let out a yell and cling tighter to each other. Mud and debris covered their faces and plastered their eyes shut.

The side of the mountain moved faster and faster, and suddenly they were falling through mid-air. Their hearts jumped into their throats as they realized they would soon be dashed to their deaths. A calmness fell over them as the crushing noise of the mountain was left behind and only the whirring of the wind brushed their ears.

They grasped each other tighter when suddenly a great concussion hit their bodies, knocking all the wind from their lungs. For an instant they thought they had died, but then they felt water rushing over them, even into their mouths and mud-caked noses. The young boy kept his eyes shut and kicked his legs instinctively, realizing he was in water and could drown. He kicked and kicked, all the time hanging onto the young girl.

His lungs were burning when he finally felt air on his face and opened his mouth to inhale the much-needed air.

"Breathe!" he yelled to the girl. "Breathe!"

She spit out a mouthful of water and with her left hand rubbed at her eyes and face. She rubbed again, as the boy cleared his own eyes and began to focus on the small lake into which they had fallen.

"We're alive! Try to float; I'll pull you," he shouted as he swam and splashed water on his face to clear the mud away from his nose and eyes.

"Yes, we're alive," she said softly as she tried to mimic his swimming and take deep breaths of air.

The two near sacrifices of Jaguar Paw swam to the edge of

the pond to a stand of reeds on the marshy end. They were soon struggling to their feet and walking up on dry land. The rain had stopped. As they sat down on the bank, they looked up the side of the mountain from where they had just fallen in the landslide.

A brown line showed the muddy trail that had fallen under their weight, and they couldn't believe their good fortune to have fallen into the small lake instead of onto the rocks all around them.

The boy looked at the girl and spoke.

"My name is Bird Jaguar."

"My name is Zak Kuk. I am the daughter of a loyal servant of Jaguar Paw," she replied.

"I am the son of Scroll Squirrel, a warrior of Jaguar Paw," Bird Jaguar replied.

The two sat and looked at each other, the mud now washed from their bodies. The young boy was still covered with patches of Mayan Blue. They were cut and bleeding all over their bodies from their slide down the mountain. Wracked with obvious pain, neither could adjust to what had just happened, beginning with their near deaths in the cenote, the underground lake that provided their escape, followed by their race from the warriors of Tikal. But now they were alive, their leaders killed, and their families probably dead.

"I went north with my father last year to trade for jade. The people were very nice. I didn't see any blue slaves," Bird Jaguar said.

"No slaves?" Zak Kuk asked.

"I didn't see any. I even got to look at the stars through a great building on top of a temple," Bird Jaguar said, wiping blood from his nose.

"Today, I was also chosen to go to the stars. To die and escort a great one into the heavens," Zak Kuk said and looked down at her bruised hands.

"Were you ready?" Bird Jaguar asked.

"I think so. But now that I am still alive, I don't know," Zak Kuk replied.

"I know how to live in the forest and Tikal is to the south of Calakmul. We should try to reach Palenque or the great lake to the north or east," the boy said. "We must be careful and not become slaves or our escape would have been worthless."

"I guess I'm not ready to die . . . to have my heart cut out for the gods," Zak Kuk said and began to cry. "I want to live."

"Then live we shall," Bird Jaguar said. He rose to his feet and reached out for her hand.

She took it, stood up, and wiped her tears away. She stood a head taller than he was.

Without speaking, they walked around the small lake until they found an animal path that led down and away from the mountain. The boy noticed a red plant with small flowers and broke off one of its limbs. He took the oozing sap of the plant and began to rub it on the cuts on his arms and face. He immediately felt relief from the pain. The girl did the same. They turned back to the small path and soon they were deep in the rainforest, in search of something they had never known: a life without fear of a god who would rather see them dead than alive.

1

Jaguar

In the rainforest west of Lubaantun, Belize, Ryan O'Keefe MacGregor held on to a rope tightly as the pulley wheel whined from his weight on the line. The 300-pound jaguar raced through the jungle below him, looking up and never losing him in her sight. His knuckles were white from the strain of his tight grasp. His right canvas boot was locked into a rope stirrup to balance his body on the rainforest trolley system.

He could see the changeover ahead and readied himself to leap to the large branch and grab the rope for the next ride through the second-tier canopy of the rainforest. The branch approached, and he shifted on the rope, let go precisely on time, and took a leap of faith with the next lunge forward.

The jaguar sprinted up the tree and swiped at R.O. with her claws, just missing his head but slamming into his back-pack at full speed. The force of the collision pushed R.O. onto the downhill slope of the trolley and away from her potentially deadly second swing.

R.O. looked back and took a deep breath knowing that the jaguar would race back down the tree and follow him through the forest with all her might. He heard the meow of her cub in his pack again, and so did the mother.

She snarled and jumped down to another tree to get under him faster, hoping to sink her large canine teeth into the skull of this young human and tear him limb from limb. She would then nurse her cub and eat the boy, all at the same time.

The next junction of the hanging trolley system, which scientists had built to traverse great distances through the rainforest, came up quickly. R.O. quickly unfastened his safety belt to latch it onto the next section, firmly putting his right boot into the next stirrup, when suddenly he sensed something dangerously close.

He looked to his right and the jaguar was almost to his platform so he jumped out without hooking up to the next line. He hung on for dear life. The female jaguar leaped from the limb and swiped at his face with her claws fully extended. He twisted as much as he could, but a claw caught the top of his right ear ripping a half-inch hole in the cartilage.

"Ow!" R.O. screamed as the jaguar landed on a large branch just behind him.

She lunged again, but he was off and moving through the air. The large cat landed on a limb five feet below him. She ran to the end of the limb and jumped, clawing wildly in the air and raking the back of his left boot before falling to the floor of the jungle below. Cushioned by the rich foliage, the jaguar landed with a loud thud.

As R.O. moved quickly through the air, blood ran down his neck and all over his shirt and shorts. The mother jaguar rose to her feet and tried to steady herself before again running after the human who had taken her cub.

R.O. could see another trolley exchange ahead and heard voices. He reached down to his vest with his free hand and found the lanyard with his whistle on the end. Finally biting down on the whistle, he blew it with all of his might. He soon heard a return whistle and took a deep breath, knowing that his big brother Chris was dead ahead.

The mother jaguar ran wildly beneath him, keeping pace with the speed of the gliding trolley. He then blew three sharp blasts on the whistle to let his brother know he was coming in "hot," or in trouble, as his mother would like to say. He looked ahead for the next exchange as he whizzed through the air some forty feet above the floor of the forest. The mother jaguar had gained on R.O., but he couldn't see her.

The exchange was straight ahead and R.O. prepared to jump to the limb, because he didn't have to unhook the harness. It would be a clean change over. He reached out with his left hand, when suddenly he felt a warm, hairy body slam into him and knock him loose from the trolley apparatus. He wildly felt for the rope but missed it, plunging to a limb below and landing on his stomach, knocking the wind out of his lungs.

He choked to suck in air, when he saw the big cat standing right in front of him, her yellow eyes glaring and her white teeth exposed in a ferocious snarl. She growled slowly, knowing she had cornered her prey. The hackles on her neck were standing straight-up; her ears were laid back ready for an attack. She moved warily on the limb, knowing her cub was hidden somewhere inside this human but not understanding where.

She inched closer and closer as R.O. lifted his right leg over the limb so he wouldn't fall, still trying to catch his breath. The big cat let out a screeching growl.

"Oh no," R.O. said softly.

"Be real still," said a voice from above, even softer than his. "How did you get this cat so mad at you?" Chris asked softly, as he lowered a rope down to where it lay on the limb next to R.O.

The mother jaguar now looked up at Chris and screamed as loud as she could. It echoed through the rainforest.

"She's really mad, Chris. I was playing with her cub and when she came back, I got scared and put it in my pack," R.O. said.

"You did *what?*" Chris exclaimed. "You are one huge

lamebrain. But I'll save that for later after I let her eat you."

"Wait, I didn't mean to do it. I just panicked," R. O. replied softly.

"Where's the cub now?" Chris asked.

The mother cat adjusted her posture as she assessed her new problem with two humans in front of her. Her low, guttural growl kept pace with her movements. She was ready to attack, regardless of the odds.

"Take the rope and tie it to your pack, slowly. Then unzip it so she can see her cub. Do it now," Chris commanded.

R.O. moved as quickly as he could. The jaguar was now only eight feet away and inching closer for an attack. Her claws could rip his skin to shreds in just a few seconds and her canines could pierce his skull in one bite.

With the rope secured to the pack, R.O. carefully felt for the zipper, never taking his eyes off the big cat. When he found the right one, he pulled it open and instantly the tiny black cub's head popped out, as it gave out a big meow. The mother lunged forward, but Chris pulled the pack sideways into the air causing the mother to change her course away from R.O. and toward the pack.

In one big swing, Chris slung the pack toward the jungle below. The mother jumped from limb to limb to keep up with the movement of the pack until it was resting in the bushes below. With one quick tear of her paws, she freed her cub. The mother turned toward the boys above, as if warning them to stay away, and gave out a blood-chilling scream. She then picked up the cub with her teeth and took off in a run into the forest.

Chris lowered himself to R.O. and helped him sit up on the limb.

"Looks like she got the better of you, little brother," Chris said, eyeing the blood that had spilled everywhere. "You'll need a few stitches for that wound."

"Well, I could have gotten away," R.O. said as he felt the gash and clotted blood on his ear.

"Maybe you could have, but she would have left more than a hole in your ear," Chris replied.

He opened a side pocket of his trusty safari vest and brought out a tube of ointment and his water bottle. He poured water over the wound and dried it off with a red bandana he took from his pack.

"Here. Rub this over the cut so you don't get any infections. Those jaguar claws are known to carry lots of nasty bacteria. It might rot your ear right off. But then you would have a story to tell about our trip with the folks, wouldn't you?" Chris said and smiled.

"You always try to scare me into doing something. I'll do it because I know it's the best thing to do, not because you told me to do it," R.O. said and winced as he touched the cut with the clear gel ointment on his fingers.

"Is that the only spot she got you? You look like you were bit all over," Chris asked.

"Yup," R. O. replied as he kept applying the ointment. "She wouldn't have gotten there if I hadn't taken so long in the last change over. I kept looking for her and that slowed me down."

"You know what I'm going to say, don't you?" Chris declared.

"Yes. 'Never look behind when you're running from something. It will only slow you down and if they're going to catch you, they're going to catch you,'" R.O. replied.

"Very good. Now let's go find the girls. They're out here somewhere," Chris said.

"You let Natalie and Heather go off by themselves?" R.O. asked as he stood up on the fourteen-inch limb and steadied his balance, trying to not look down to the ground forty feet below.

"Yes, I told them I would go find you and then we would go exploring together. Pretty glad I came! You know Dr. Phelps, the Norwegian archaeologist? He said there were several temples still out here that had never been dug out. I thought it would be fun to check them out before we have to meet up with Mom and Dad. You don't remember the plan?" Chris said and looked at R.O. worriedly.

"Yes, I remember. I was just thinking about the jaguar and her cub. I didn't mean to make her mad," R.O. said.

"Look, that was one of the first things Dad taught us about nature. Never mess with the young of any species of animals. It's either harmful to them or dangerous to us, or both," Chris replied.

"I know. I just forgot when I started playing with the cub. I won't do it again," R.O. said with a somber look on his face.

"O.K., now shake it off and let's go have some fun," Chris said, then he snapped R.O.'s harness to the next section of the trolley system.

They both leaned into the ropes and soon they were sailing through the second canopy of the rainforest as beautiful trees and birds passed by.

Within a few minutes, they could hear Natalie, Chris's girlfriend, and Heather, their sister, laughing and talking. One more exchange on the primitive pulley and rope system and they were in view of the two girls.

"What *happened* to you?" Heather exclaimed as she saw the dried blood all over R.O.'s clothes.

"Well, I, I . . . " R. O. started.

"He was playing with a jaguar cub when the mother came home," Chris interrupted.

"What an idiot," Heather quickly said.

"Well, I wouldn't be so hard on him," Natalie said and patted his cheek. "I would just say that whatever good sense he had, he left it in New Guinea last month!"

"Gee, thanks, Natalie," R.O. replied.

"Look what we found, Chris," Heather said with a big smile on her face.

"Well, we didn't exactly discover it, but it was exactly where Dr. Phelps said it would be," Natalie added.

"The temple, I see. Have you been inside or climbed to the top yet?" Chris asked, examining the stone structure behind them.

"No, we were waiting for you and little brother here, the jaguar tamer," Heather said and laughed. "Is Mom going to be mad at you or what?"

"Enough of the taunting. His ear will be his souvenir for doing something less than smart. Some people do stupid things and never live to regret it," Chris said and took off his harness for the trolley system. "Get your packs on and tighten up your boots. We're going to climb this thing," he said and stepped from the tree limb to the rocky surface of the temple.

The Mayan temple was more than a thousand years old, and overgrown with nearly as many years of jungle growth. Full-sized trees had grown up and died dozens of times in this tropical rainforest and had wormed their way into the rocky crevices of the ancient building. Chris got a good footing, reached out, and pulled the others toward him onto the ancient stone steps.

"Lean into the steps and watch for snakes on the overhanging limbs," Chris ordered and began to climb.

Natalie, age eighteen, was first behind him, her long auburn hair tied back in a tight braid to avoid tangling on the tree limbs. Heather, age fourteen, had her blonde hair tucked inside a Texas Rangers baseball cap. R.O., age thirteen, was last and was constantly looking back for the mad mother jaguar.

"Chris, this reminds me of the giant tree root in China," Natalie said, referring to the tree that had roots more than a hundred feet long that had penetrated into a cave and provided a natural ladder for escape to the surface.

"Yes, pretty close, but with lots of daylight filtering through the canopy. I see a break in the trees just ahead," Chris replied.

They all worked their way through the thick foliage,

struggling to find their footing on the ancient stone temple that was covered with vines and roots.

"Wow. You should see this," Chris suddenly exclaimed.

Natalie pushed up through the tree branches to stand on the stairs next to him.

"What is it?" she asked, as Heather soon joined them.

"It's a face carved into the side of the temple," Chris replied.

"It's a Mayan god. If you look around you'll probably find the hieroglyph that explains who he is," R.O. said from behind them.

"Well, that homework Mom assigned after New Guinea is paying off," Heather said.

"I knew it before then, if you don't mind," R.O. snapped back.

"Cool it," Chris said quickly. "It's a good clue. Let's keep moving."

The four teens were soon out of the top of the trees and side-stepping small bushes and plant debris as they reached the summit of the temple, which was the height of a ten-story building.

"What a magnificent view!" Natalie said first, as all soon agreed.

"I had lost track of time, but it is straight-up noon. It looks near dark under the rainforest canopy," Heather said.

"Now it's going to get hot," R.O. added.

"What did Dr. Phelps name this place?" Natalie asked.

"He called it Nim Li Punit. Built around 700 A.D. and abandoned about 1,200 A.D. It's quite amazing. If it were cleaned and dug out like the other ancient Mayan ruins, it would be magnificent," Chris replied.

"What are all these holes over here?" R.O. asked.

The other three teens walked across the top of the temple mount to where R.O. was standing.

"Looters," Natalie said.

"Too bad. Looks like they dug everywhere," Heather replied.

"And they hit pay dirt on this hole," Chris said. "Pottery shards are everywhere, so they must have dug into a cache of something and broke it up while digging."

"Archaeologists would have loved to have found it first," Natalie said.

"Look at this hole," R.O. said and disappeared down into it.

"Wait!" Chris yelled.

"Too late, big brother," Heather said. "Let's just leave him in it for awhile to teach him a lesson."

"Can't do that. I would like to, but you know," Chris said and stepped into the six-foot-wide hole that descended into blackness below.

Chris took out his flashlight, put on his leather utility gloves, and pointed the light ahead of him. He soon was sliding on his bottom deeper into the hole.

"Ryan!" he shouted, but heard no answer.

Chris felt a kick in his back and turned to find Natalie right behind him. She smiled so that he wouldn't chastise her for following him.

"Where's Heather?" he asked.

"I'm right behind Natalie. You're not leaving me up there by myself. What if R.O.'s jaguar mama came looking for revenge?" she joked.

They moved further into the wide, dirt hole before coming to a stone wall with an opening only two feet in diameter.

"He didn't go in there, did he?" Natalie said incredulously.

"I'm afraid he did," Chris replied.

"Well, I'm not going down there," Heather said.

"Then you two will have to wait here by yourselves and hope an earthquake doesn't dislodge twenty tons of dirt on your head," Chris said.

"I'll be behind Natalie," Heather said adjusting her Rangers cap. Natalie turned on a flashlight she pulled from her cargo shorts.

Chris took off his backpack, flattened it as much as he could, and then shimmied through the hole, his flashlight in his left hand. When he had disappeared, Natalie turned to Heather and winked.

"Here's courage," she said as she pulled her gloves on tighter and disappeared into the hole.

Heather didn't even wait for Natalie's boots to disappear before she went in right behind her. The earthen hole that had led them into the bowels of the ancient Mayan temple was now totally black.

2

The Cenote

"Heather, let go of my boot," Natalie said inside the stone tunnel.

"It's pretty dark in here. I don't want to lose you," Heather said, as she spit out the dirt from her mouth.

"Calm down, ladies. We haven't made a turn in here yet," Chris said. "Well, I spoke too soon. We've got a choice up here between two tunnels, one goes up and one goes down," Chris said.

"I bet the little twerp went down," Natalie said, venting some anger.

"I wouldn't have been as nice as that," Heather quickly responded about Natalie's comment.

"Down we go," Chris replied. "It's a bigger tunnel."

"That's really encouraging," Heather said sarcastically.

Chris turned on his side and repositioned his pack. As the leader of the teens and eldest son of the MacGregor family, he always took it upon himself to pack most of the survival gear they would need in any wilderness environment. Once situated in the new tunnel, he found he could sit up and avoid tearing up his knees further. Within ten feet, he could almost stand up. Soon the three teens were all standing together in a room that was ten-feet high and lined with stones. At the end of the room was a small doorway about five-feet tall.

"I am so going to kill him when we find him," Heather said as she took a tissue from her pack and blotted a cut on her right knee. "I would have gladly worn long pants and knee pads if I had known we were going caving."

"I wouldn't have come. The pool back at the resort looked pretty nice to me," Natalie said honestly.

"Oh yeah, me too," Heather joined in.

"Well, obviously the ancient Mayans weren't very tall, so squat down if you can't make the clearance," Chris said and stepped into the doorway.

"Only R.O. could fit in this hole," Heather said, disgusted, as she brushed away a large spider web. "I really hate spiders."

"Spiders? Did you see one?" Natalie quickly turned around shining her flashlight in all directions.

"That's my eyes, thank you," Chris said. "I haven't seen any spiders. If I do, I will be happy to point it out before it lands in your hair and begins nesting behavior."

"Chris, you are such a, well, you know," Heather said and looked back once again.

"O.K., I've reached another step down. There is water in this one, so don't be surprised." Chris said.

"Oh, now we get wet feet," Heather moaned again.

"We must be below the water table for the rainforest," Natalie said.

"I see a light ahead," Chris said. "We may have caught up with him."

"Let me move ahead. I want to be the first to knock him out," Heather said loudly.

Chris sloshed through the shallow water before reaching a stone step that took him up and into another chamber where they found R.O. sitting on a stone ledge.

"What took you so long?" R.O. said and smiled.

Chris gave him a cold stare.

"Ryan, have you lost your mind?" Natalie asked as she entered the room.

Heather came in last and walked straight over to him.

"I would slap your face if I didn't think that Mom would ground me for a month after she buries you," Heather said.

"Hold on," Chris said and stepped between them. "What were you doing down here?"

"Well, I was just curious. I have been the finder of great treasure, you know. So I thought, what the heck, maybe I'll get lucky this time, too," R.O. said matter-of-factly.

"Well the looters beat you to it, so it's time to go," Chris said.

"There's another way out of here, you know," R.O. said.

"How do you know that, genius?" Heather said.

"I could hear people's voices that way," R.O. said and pointed down a long corridor, beyond the stone ledge.

"People? What people?" Natalie asked quickly.

"I don't know. They speak Spanish or something like it," R.O. said. "When I heard them, I decided to wait because Chris speaks pretty good Spanish."

Chris walked over to the entrance of the corridor and motioned for everyone to stop talking. He listened for a minute and then nodded his head up and down.

"Let's move quietly and I'll see if I can understand what they're saying," Chris said and stepped into the next tunnel.

Soon all the teens were inside the tunnel and moving slowly. Chris had told Natalie and R.O. to turn off their flashlights and he had turned his off too. The foreign voices became louder and then suddenly the teens felt the strangers were right on top of them. Light and shadows came from another chamber as Chris edged closer to listen.

"Dig here. There. I saw the gold there," one of the voices said in Spanish.

"This ain't near big enough for a king's tomb," another voice said.

"I didn't say it was a king. What about a queen?" the man said.

Chris turned and could see the wide-eyed anticipation of Natalie, Heather, and R.O., waiting for him to say something.

"Looters," he said softly.

"What? I can't hear you." R.O. said in a normal voice that echoed through the chamber.

The voices of the looters stopped.

"What was that?" one of them asked.

"No, it wasn't a ghost," another voice said quickly as if talking to someone somewhere else.

"I hear someone coming," Chris whispered and motioned for them to turn around and move back into the tunnel.

"Who's in there?" asked a gruff voice, as a light was shone toward the four teens.

"We're explorers," Chris said quickly.

"Keep the loot. We won't bother you," R.O. said.

"Shut up," Heather barked at him.

The man stepped back into the other chamber and shouted out in Spanish, "Toss me a gun. We've got competition down here. They must have come in through the sink hole."

Chris thought quickly and noticed handholds and steps on the wall to his right that led into blackness. He knew his group would be caught quickly and shot like rats on the run if they went back into the tunnel. Their only hope was this unknown Mayan wall.

"Up, quickly," he said to the others and began to climb.

Within seconds, the four teens were ten feet up the wall. They were twenty feet up when the man came back into the chamber brandishing a rifle followed by another man with a pistol. Seeing the empty chamber, they moved on into the water-logged tunnel in pursuit of the teens, never bothering to look up.

"Keep climbing," Chris ordered quietly. Soon he had his pack to his side as they reached a face of the wall that forced them to press against another wall of the temple.

Chills of fear crept over him as he felt the wall pressing closer and closer. He hoped they would soon reach the top of the wall when he suddenly felt a wave of air on his face. Stopping, he reached for his flashlight on his belt and turned it on. He found an open tunnel about four feet in diameter in front of his face. Crawling up and inside, he pulled Natalie into the tunnel, and then helped Heather and R.O. They all sat still for a moment and just listened.

"Who brought a water bottle?" Chris asked.

"I did," Heather whispered.

"I did, too," Natalie said.

"Break them out and let's get a big drink. This heat is sapping our strength. But we must be back above the ground level, because the temperature has gone up," Chris said and took a big gulp on Natalie's bottle.

R.O. didn't complain as he usually did when he shared the bottle with Heather.

"Well, let's go," Chris directed as he again crouched to follow the tunnel's gradual slope.

After walking for fifteen minutes, the four teens stopped and stared at a trickle of light that leaked in from the surface. Without talking, they started their last climb up the narrow passage toward the light. Reaching the end, Chris could see there were several rocks or boulders stacked over the mouth of the tunnel with sunlight penetrating through the cracks.

"What now?" Natalie asked working her way up next to him. "You could use a shower, big boy," she added, which made him smile.

"I'm sure we all could," Chris said.

"I'm not going back down," Heather said.

"We are if we can't push those boulders out of the way," R.O. said.

Chris took his knife from his belt and tried to wedge it between some of the rocks. Centuries of packed dirt began to fall back toward the foursome.

"Hey," Heather said as dirt fell in her face.

"Close your eyes. Chris is trying to dig at the rocks," Natalie said to R.O. and Heather.

"Man, do I ever miss the monsoon rains of New Guinea, right now," Heather replied.

The earth around them moved.

"What was that?" Natalie asked anxiously.

"What was what?" Chris replied. He had not felt the movement because of his digging.

The earth moved again, and the rocks around them jolted downward as if they were in a rock-and-earthen elevator.

"I felt *that*!" Chris exclaimed. "Hang on! I think this tunnel must be some kind of chute, used for moving rocks to build this temple."

The earth moved again and the floor under the teens dropped three feet away from the tiny hole that Chris had been digging.

"Chris, I'm scared," Heather said softly, as if she were afraid her words would make it worse.

Natalie reached out for her hand, but the rock shaft moved again, and didn't stop for a full three seconds. R.O. was jarred loose from his hold on the wall and slid down into the hole.

"Chris, Ryan!" Natalie yelled.

"I see him," Chris replied.

"R.O., turn on your light!" Chris yelled.

There was no sound and no light.

The earth moved again, and the shaft, cemented together by a thousand years of debris, fell through the center of the temple, bypassing hidden chambers and rooms until suddenly the kids were free-falling through space in darkness. The roar of the rock slide was all around them. Suddenly, their rapid movement was slowed when they hit water, hard. They were so surprised that they did not think to take a breath of air as they plunged deep into an underground lake, rocks falling all around them.

Chris began flailing in the water, trying to swim to the

surface. A rock, about four-inches wide, hit him on the shoulder. Natalie reached out and found his leg and began pulling herself to the surface, spitting out mouthfuls of water and choking hard.

"Chris," she yelled over the echo of the rock slide in the cavern around them.

"Tread water. Cover your head," Chris yelled back and felt around for his flashlight on his utility belt.

Once he had the flashlight in his hand, he flipped the switch and found Natalie right away. She had a cut above her right eye. Then he spotted Heather's blonde hair floating in the water.

"Heather's hurt," he yelled and swam quickly to her, as the last of the rock shaft pelted the water around them.

He reached out, turned her over quickly in the water, and squeezed under her arms. With no solid ground to use for resuscitation, he quickly decided he would try a Heimlich maneuver in the water. He had no idea if it would work but he made one quick squeeze and Heather belched out a mouthful of water, and then choked in some air.

Natalie had reached them and was holding the flashlight so Chris could work with Heather. The flashlight cord was still tightly fastened around her wrist.

"Heather, *Heather,*" Chris said repeatedly until she finally opened her eyes.

"My head hurts so bad," she finally said.

"Good, I'm glad you're alive to feel it," Chris said and felt around her blonde hair until he found a bump about the size of a chicken egg.

Heather put her hand on Chris' hand and spoke.

"Don't touch it. It really hurts," she said.

"You're lucky it didn't go inside your head. There were some pretty big rocks to dodge," Natalie said.

"What about Ryan?" Heather said groggily.

"I almost forgot. He came down first," Chris said, a worried expression on his face.

"Look, over there!" Natalie exclaimed pointing to a light moving around on the edge of the underground lake.

Chris felt around his vest and found his whistle. Quickly putting it in his mouth he blew two long bursts. He got two back quickly.

"That's a relief," Natalie said.

"Let's swim that way," Chris replied and pulled Heather through the water, talking to her the whole time.

In a few moments, they had reached the sandy shoreline where R.O. was sitting, shining his flashlight around.

"Give me a hand," Chris shouted to R.O.

He quickly jumped up and grabbed Heather's left shoulder and helped Chris pull her out of the water, laying her flat on the sand.

"Thanks, little brother," Heather said and tried to smile but frowned and grabbed the bump on her head.

"I think she's got a mild concussion," Chris said and sat down.

He took his small flashlight and leaned over her.

"I'm going to shine this into your eyes, so don't close them. Just look past me," he said to Heather.

Moving the light across her eyes, he then sat back down.

"She's fine. No brain damage," Chris said.

"Wait, I've always thought she was brain damaged," R.O. popped off.

"Ryan, shut up," Natalie said.

"I didn't mean it personally," R.O. replied.

"R.O., can it!" Chris said sharply.

"Where'd you learn that?" Natalie asked Chris.

"The Royal Australian Navy Camp. They taught us how to recognize a dilated pupil to check for severe brain damage when in the field," Chris replied. "We learned how to field dress wounds and to do stitches."

"I'm impressed," Heather said quietly.

"What now?" R.O. said.

"Well, you obviously came down with the bottom of the

shoot. But why are your shoes blue?" Chris asked, as he noticed R.O.'s feet for the first time.

"I don't know. The bottom layer of the rock chute was right on top of me and when I hit the water it drove me all the way to the sandy bottom. I was stuck in the bottom up to my knees. I used the rocks all around me to wedge my way out. That's when I swam to the surface, but I must have come up out of the way because I could still hear rocks hitting the water all around me. So I started swimming really hard in the pitch dark. I was afraid I would hit a rock wall or something, and then my knees touched the sand and I crawled up on the beach," R.O. explained.

"How are you feeling?" Chris asked Heather.

"My head is still pounding but I can focus on you and see you O.K.," she replied.

"Let's try standing up," Chris said and stood up, still holding her right hand.

"O.K., I'll try," she replied and started leaning forward slowly.

Natalie was under one shoulder and Chris under the other as Heather climbed to her feet. She stood and then touched the bump on her head.

"I feel better than I thought I would," she replied.

"What was that we fell through?" Natalie asked and shone her light at the hole in the ceiling of the cavern.

"Some sort of a chute, maybe used to build the temple. There had to be a reason the temple connected to this water down here," Chris said and pointed his light to the same spot. "But I do know we can't stay down here. We'll have to climb our way out."

"O.K., so where do we start?" Natalie asked.

"Over there," answered R.O., who was pointing his light at a hole in the ceiling about twenty feet up from the water's edge.

"I don't think we have any ropes," Heather said, looking at R.O.

"I'll check it out," Chris said and starting walking along the beach.

As he approached the wall, he noticed several hieroglyphs carved about ten-feet up. To the side of the glyphs were foot- and hand-holds that had been chiseled out of the stone. He jogged back to the others with the good news.

"There are hand-holds that lead up to the entrance with lots of Mayan glyphs on each side. Looks like that was the way out even a thousand years ago," he said.

"What a relief," Heather said.

"Hope there's daylight on the other side," R.O. added.

They all looked at him and frowned for bringing up the obvious, but unwanted, thought at the present.

Chris led the others to the wall. He watched Heather as she regained her normal gait and balance.

"R.O., you're first. But when you get in, you stop and wait for me. If you take off again, I promise I will pay for your way back to Texas tomorrow. Got it?" Chris said firmly.

"I got it," R.O. said.

As R.O. began to climb, Heather noticed his shoes for the first time.

"How'd you get blue shoes?" she asked loudly.

"He hit the sandy bottom and said it was solid blue," Natalie replied.

"That's weird," Heather replied.

The four teens made the climb without effort, because the carved-out hand-holds were engineered for people who were about a foot shorter than they were. Once inside the small opening at the top, Chris led them into a small tunnel that was free of debris, despite the shifting of the rocky chute.

"Natalie, take up the rear and keep Heather in front of you," Chris said softly as his voice echoed through the tunnel.

After about ten feet, the passageway narrowed and began to steepen, until they were again climbing straight up an ancient wall. The round stones of the wall were made for bare feet and made their climbing boots slip, leading to cuts and skinned knees.

"Ow," Natalie said as she endured another cut on her legs.

"I can see a chamber just above us," Chris said. He climbed into the passageway, reached down, and pulled the others in one at a time.

Heather walked across the chamber to where she could see a crack of light coming through the rocks.

"I can see blue sky," she said.

"That's what it is," Chris said and looked up.

He took his long knife from his belt and poked around at the opening. He started moving along the wall, feeling each protruding rock or uneven crevasse. When he had walked ten feet, he stopped.

"R.O., come over here," he said. "Put your hands here," he demonstrated by putting his hands over two protruding stones. "When I say push, then push with all of your might."

"Can I help?" Natalie said and came over.

"You take one and R.O. will take the other," Chris said and walked back to where he had been standing ten feet away.

He put his knife in a crease in the wall and held it with both hands.

"Ready? One, two, three—push!" he shouted.

R.O. leaned into the stone, but it didn't move. Natalie got her stone to budge only after groaning and yelling at it.

R.O.'s stone began to move as Chris pushed his nine-inch-knife deep into the crease and leaned against the butt of the knife with both hands.

"Push! Keep pushing," Chris yelled.

Heather ran over to R.O., put her hands around his, and pushed harder.

Chris's knife began to slide downward, making a screeching noise as the steel rubbed against the stone. The wall began to move and sand started to flow into the room from the creases between all the stones.

"Oh my gosh. Chris, what are we doing?" Heather shouted over the noise.

"I think the wall is moving," Natalie shouted.

More sand poured into the room until the wall stopped moving.

"That's it," Chris said. "It slid back about a foot. There's enough room for us to leave. I think it's a secret escape route for the king and his family."

He picked up his flashlight and walked to the corner of the room where the one-foot opening now existed.

"Let's see where it goes," he said and stepped into darkness and out of sight.

"I'm not waiting here," Heather said, picking up her flashlight and quickly following Chris. R.O. and Natalie were right behind her.

3

The Dirigible

Chris felt his way along the narrow corridor until Heather bumped into him from behind.

"Sorry," Heather said.

"That's O.K. How's your head?" he asked.

"Better, the double vision has gone away."

Chris turned around and shined the light in her face.

"Double vision? You didn't say anything about double vision," Chris said.

"Hey, don't shine that in my face. I was just kidding. Just wanted to see if you still love me," Heather said and smiled.

"No, he loves me," Natalie said with a smile as she entered the light bubble that their flashlights were creating.

"I don't love anybody, so step aside and let the great explorer pass," R.O. said as he tried to push his way through.

"No so fast, little buddy," Chris said and put his right hand on R.O.'s head. "You're the caboose on this train today."

R.O. knew when not to question Chris' authority and this was one of those times.

Natalie moved close to Chris and gave him a quick kiss on the mouth and smiled.

"Oh, please. I thought I could go all day without that," R.O. said.

The four teens began to move through the corridor for about twenty minutes before they reached a dead end.

"Looks like the only way is up," Chris said as he looked upward at a black chimney over their heads. "There are plenty of hand-holds, so grab carefully and don't pull any rocks lose. We don't want to take any chances and create another chute falling into the lake."

"That's a roger for sure, Captain," Heather said and lightly rubbed the knot on her head.

Chris took the lead once again and began to climb. The teens didn't talk the entire time while they worked their way upward. They all put their small flashlights in their mouths or on their utility belts, pointing upward.

"O.K., I'm up and in a chamber. Keep climbing," Chris called down the vertical tunnel to the others.

Soon they were all up in the chamber, huffing and trying to catch their breath.

"I must be out of shape," Natalie was the first to comment.

"No. You're just using different muscles than we have the past few months," Chris responded and began to walk around the room. He found a tree root sticking through the wall, and again he took out his knife and began to dig. R.O. got the idea and came over and started to dig, too. Natalie joined them while Heather sat down and held her head in her hands, trying to ease the pain from her headache.

"There's light!" R.O. said as he broke through.

The other two began to dig harder and soon the afternoon sun was shining brightly through a two-foot window they had carved.

"Me first," R.O. said as he hoisted himself up and through.

Chris was the last one through after he helped Heather. The four teens now stood on top of the temple, gazing across the top of the third-tier of the rainforest canopy, more than one hundred feet in the air.

"Wait a second. We're not on the pyramid that we started on," Natalie said as she walked around.

"You're right. It's over there," Chris replied, looking across the canopy at the first pyramid.

"Oh my gosh. You're saying that we fell into the lake underneath that one, then we crawled up to the base of the pyramid, then followed an escape tunnel to this pyramid, and then climbed to the top?" Heather surmised.

"You got it, big sister!" R.O. exclaimed. "Man, we are the explorers today, and it was all because of my leading us through the shaft."

"Yes, and almost getting us killed by looters," Chris added.

Suddenly, the sun was blocked and the temples fell into a great shadow. Heather looked up and shaded her eyes from the glare coming from the dark object over their heads. No one said a word for two minutes as the object moved slowly through the sky and began to descend on top of them.

"Chris, what is it?" Natalie said as she instinctively crouched next to the top of the pyramid temple.

"Aliens!" R.O. exclaimed.

"I don't know yet," Chris answered quietly as he moved around the top of the temple, gazing upward and then down to the rainforest all around them.

"It looks like it's a big patch-work of netting," Heather said, now standing up and gazing skyward.

"You're right. It's all one big net, but what is it?" Natalie said, getting to her feet.

Suddenly, an opening the size of a small door appeared and a rope was dropped all the way to the top of the pyramid.

"Hey, Chris," Heather exclaimed as a man appeared in the opening, jumped through, and began to repel to the temple.

In a few seconds he was standing next to the four teens whose mouths were agape from what they had just witnessed. The man released his repelling harness and stepped toward them.

"I'm Dr. David North, chief archaeologist for the Camp Itzam Na team. We're setting up camp on top of the rainforest, and you are?" asked the man in the khaki shorts, brown boots, khaki shirt, and St. Louis Cardinals baseball cap.

"I'm Chris MacGregor, and this is my sister Heather, my brother R.O., and my friend Natalie Crosswhite."

"Nice to meet all of you," Dr. North said in his deep voice like a radio announcer.

"That was a cool descent," R.O. said and reached out to shake his hand.

"Thanks, mountaineering is my second love after digging up old tombs and temples," Dr. North replied. "Our ride is in a holding pattern as our team runs some tests on the rain-forest canopy to pick just the right spot to set down."

"You're going to put that big thing on top of the trees?" Heather asked.

"Exactly. We will set down slowly and carefully, so that we only cause a minimal amount of damage and then we'll operate out of the camp for the next three months," Dr. North replied. "Would you like to check it out while we wait?" he asked.

"Oh boy, would I!" R.O. exclaimed.

"Good, I'll radio for a hoist," Dr. North said and took out his transmitter.

"Camp Captain, this is Dr. North. I've got four visitors to come up," he said.

"That's a copy. Be ready for the hoist on your mark. Craven out."

Two more ropes were dropped down to the temple along with four climbing harnesses. R.O. was the first to strap one on, followed by Heather and Natalie.

"I'll wait til last," Chris said. He stared around at the beautiful view and up to the dark side of the aircraft he couldn't quite envision.

In a matter of minutes, the three teens had disappeared through the hole of the netting, while Dr. North walked around and examined the glyphs on the top of the temple.

"How many are there on your team?" Chris asked.

"We have two botanists, two zoologists, and four archaeologists. The biologists study the rainforest from the top down and we study it from the ground up, so to speak," Dr. North said just as two ropes were dropped back to the top of the pyramid. "Our turn," he said as he handed Chris the harness.

In a few seconds, Chris was lifted from the top of the pyramid. As he gazed at the panorama of beauty all around him, he thought how much his parents would love to see this.

"Heads up!" came the cry from above him as he reached the opening, which was just large enough for his broad shoulders.

He moved swiftly through the door, and a man and a woman swung him over to the side and away from the opening.

"Got ye' balance?" asked a quite attractive woman with a Scottish accent and red hair.

"Yes, I do," Chris replied, and took a double take at her face.

"Well, watch ye step and make it go lightly. Ye walkin' on ropes and ten layers of thick canvas. No knives are to be out and no smokin' lest we all go up in flames and die a horrible death. The head is painted red and it's over there. Instructions are inside on the wall and follow them perfectly. All the scientists have their own tents and they're off limits, laddie. Ye following me, are ya?" the Scotswoman from Kirkcaldy said and took a breath.

"Yes, I am," Chris replied, as Dr. North walked up.

"Is Dr. Hood taking care of you?" Dr. North asked. "She's a mechanical engineer and is responsible for making Camp Itzam Na function."

"Yes, very efficiently," Chris said as a lady dressed in green-khaki pants and shirt walked up.

"Hello, I'm Dr. Caradith Craven, the camp captain," she said and extended her hand.

As Chris clasped her hand, he could tell from the leathery feel of the skin that this tanned, middle-aged woman had been an outdoorsman all her life. However, her warm smile made him feel relaxed and at home.

"Dr. North is our chief scientist and Dr. Hood is our camp

supervisor and safety director. Mind Dr. Hood and you won't fall off this flying camp, kill yourself, and make your parents more than a little upset. As I said, we call this Camp Itzam Na. It's Mayan for 'the god from whom all things come.' The other translation is iguana house," Dr. Craven said. "Oh, and if you feel sick, come see me. I'm the camp doctor."

Chris finally succumbed to the compulsion to look up, and for the first time, he noticed a bright yellow blimp that was suspending the camp with steel cables.

"Wow," he said.

Dr. Craven, Dr. North, and Dr. Hood laughed.

"It's common for visitors to miss the dirigible overhead because of their concentrating on the view of the camp around them," Dr. Craven said.

"The blimp is the SS *Napoleon* out of Paris, France. We contracted her to carry our camp from the island of Cozumel, where we built it, to the top of the rainforest canopy here in the Maya Mountains," Dr. North said as Heather, Natalie, and R.O. walked up.

There was also a girl about R.O.'s height, with dark, brown hair and an equally dark tan standing next to him. R.O. appeared smitten with this thirteen-year-old-beauty, because he kept looking at her and then at Natalie and Heather, who both had sly smiles on their faces.

"I'm impressed. I'd heard of this being done in the Amazon when I was younger but had never seen a third-tier canopy camp before," Chris replied.

"Oh, and don't let me forget to introduce one of our guests," Dr. Craven said and reached out for the dark-haired girl. "This is Katelynn Komarovski. Her grandmother is the famous Russian archaeologist, Tatiana Komarovski. We thought it would be fun to have her along to see what made the Komarovski name famous. And besides, I'm good friends with her other grandparents, the Harmons."

"Nice to meet you, Katelynn," Chris said and reached out to shake her hand.

"It's a pleasure," Katelynn replied.

"O.K., now for the big question, what are you kids doing out here?" Dr. North asked.

"We were exploring some of the Mayan temples in the area and ran into some tomb raiders in the temple to the south," Chris started to explain.

"We escaped through some underground tunnels between the two temples," R.O. added.

"But that was after we nearly drowned when we fell two hundred feet through the first temple into an underground lake. My head still hurts. You guys wouldn't happen to have a Tylenol, would you?" Heather asked.

"A lake? Are you sure?" Dr. North asked.

"Positive," R.O. said. "And I've got blue shoes to prove it."

Dr. North kneeled down, rubbed his hands over the shoes, and then stood up.

"Maya Blue for sure. That's very rare, indeed. Could you show us where this was?" North asked.

"Yeah, if you want to slide on your butt down one hundred feet of rock and then plunge another hundred feet into a lake—all in the dark!" Heather said sarcastically.

Chris gave her a stern, squinted look for bad manners and jumped in. She squinted back at him.

"It was an accidental discovery. I think the vertical tunnel was a chute of some kind for delivering materials to take in or take out, and we stumbled across it during our escape," he said.

"I'll have to investigate this. Any time Maya Blue pops up on the scene, it's a big moment in archaeology in this region," Dr. North said.

"Time for descent!" called a voice over a loud speaker on the main tent in the middle of the camp.

"O.K., you kids follow me," Dr. Craven said. "We have a safe zone in the middle of the camp that is reinforced so branches won't come piercing through the canvas floor and stab you. There are only five team members here now. The rest arrive tomorrow. It's too dangerous to land with everyone in the camp."

When the kids and the five team members were situated in the middle of the camp, Dr. Craven walked over to an electronic panel that looked like the dashboard of a sophisticated roadster. She pulled a couple of levers and pushed a few buttons and a whining noise filled the air. Everyone was given a pair of hearing protectors, which they put on immediately.

"What's that?" R.O. was the first to ask.

"That's the air compressors turning on. The camp is built upon a ring of inflatable tubing that crisscrosses like the spokes of a bicycle wheel. The tubing stabilizes the net and canvas platform," Dr. Craven said loudly.

The camp began to shift, rising four feet higher in the air. The whining noise grew to a fever pitch. Soon the tubing was full of air and pressurized.

"This is amazing," Chris said and walked to the edge of the safety zone.

The dirigible lowered Camp Itzam Na down to the trees and gently began to put it in place.

"Hang on," Dr. North shouted to everyone as the flooring began to shift and slide.

The four-foot tubing began to settle in place over the trees and soon the compressors subsided their whining, because no leaks were detected. Dr. Hood led three crew-members around to the edges, and with giant wrenches they started to disassemble the couplings that attached the camp to the cables from the dirigible.

R.O. took off his hearing protectors, walked to the side of the camp, and leaned on the tubing to look down into the forest.

"This is so cool," he said.

Heather walked up behind him and gave him a teasing push forward.

"Hey, watch it," R.O. shouted.

"Oops, I'm sorry. I didn't mean to bump into you," Heather said and laughed.

Chris, tired of their fussing, just ignored both of them.

"Gosh, this is awesome," Natalie said.

"Yes, and to think my grandmother lived out there for decades trying to solve the mystery of the Mayan hieroglyphs," Katelynn said.

"She must have been very brave," Natalie replied.

"She was. She's our family hero," Katelynn added.

"Oh no!" Heather screamed.

Chris ran over to her, bouncing slightly on the rope flooring.

"What is it?" Chris asked quickly.

"Ryan fell over the side. I mean, we were playing and I pushed him maybe too hard," Heather said with a mortified look on her face.

"Where's R.O.?" Natalie asked as she ran up to them.

"Heather pushed him over the side. Let's hope he's hung up in the trees," Chris said and turned to alert the camp captain.

"I didn't mean to," Heather said as tears began to flow from her eyes.

Suddenly they heard a snickering beside one of the winches and R.O. stepped out, trying to contain his laughing.

"First she tries to kill me, then she cries about me. Heather you are so messed up," R.O. said and laughed out loud.

"Look, he has a harness around his waist," Natalie said.

"Yup, I hooked it up before she walked over and then I just crawled back up over by the wench," R.O. said with a big grin on his face.

"You mean little . . . " Heather started before Chris stepped in front of her.

"Ryan, that's mean," Natalie said.

R.O. suddenly lost his smile.

"Ditto to that, little brother. I am sure that Mom will have something to add about this demented little stunt. I wouldn't want to be in your shoes," Chris said and put his arm around Heather.

"What's going on?" Katelynn Komarovski asked as she walked up.

R.O. blushed when he saw her.

"R.O., Dr. Craven wants to look at your ear. Dr. North noticed all the clotted blood and said you might need to have stitches," she said. "How'd you hurt it?"

"Tell her to sew up his mouth while she's at it," Heather said and smiled.

"Ditto to that," Natalie said.

"I hope the needle going through your ear doesn't hurt too bad," Chris said and tried to contain his laugh.

"Are they always that mean to you?" Katelynn said.

"Worse, far worse," R.O. said. He then walked away with her toward Dr. Craven's tent.

Heather, Natalie, and Chris gave each other high fives with great joy.

4

Mr. Frost

Forty miles from Camp Itzam Na, out in the blue Caribbean Sea, the $20 million yacht the *Calakmul Queen* was floating over a giant blue hole. Two divers were boarding from the diver's platform that had been lowered five feet into the ocean and lifted to the deck by an automated, high-tech pulley system. Three attendants wearing the white uniforms of Frost Global Enterprises, Ltd., quickly helped the two divers take off the gear and toweled them dry. A tall, elegant brunette with "Emily" monogrammed above the right shirt pocket of her officer's uniform gave each man a light cotton robe.

"Excellent dive, Mr. Frost," said the tall man with the pointed chin and black eyes as he took a drink from one of the crew members.

"Yes, the Caribbean Sea is a wonderful place to find great resources," Mr. Frost said and sat down on a wicker chair with white leather cushions, drink in hand.

"But you didn't ask me to come all the way to the coast of Central America to discover what any good writer for a travel magazine could tell me, did you?" the man asked in his memorable British accent.

Mr. Frost took a drink of his strong beverage and looked up.

"No, that would be foolish, and foolishness is not one of my traits, Sir Philip," Mr. Frost replied, taking another sip. "I am looking for partners in a venture that will change the value of Mayan artifacts forever."

"Look Mr. Frost, I'm into many ventures, some good, some not so good. What would I want with old jewelry and skulls?" Sir Philip said, sounding irritated.

Mr. Frost looked across the teak deck toward the entrance of the lounge and snapped his fingers at Emily who was still standing there waiting. She walked over quickly and stopped.

"Bring out the chest," Mr. Frost said.

"Yes, sir," she replied and walked away.

In less than two minutes, two brawny men were carrying a four-foot-long aluminum chest across the deck with one man on each end. They carefully set it down on the deck between Mr. Frost and his guest.

"Sir Philip, what I have before you is something that may be worth more than all the investments you have ever made or will ever make," Mr. Frost said.

"I've got to see this," Sir Philip said sarcastically.

Mr. Frost set his drink down and leaned forward over the box. Taking a key from a gold chain on his wrist, he opened the padlock on the side and set the lock on the table next to his drink. He carefully lifted the latch and pushed the lid upward until it lay completely open. He reached in and moved the packing peanuts aside. Carefully, he lifted a jade mask from the top of the box and laid it on the table between them. The sun penetrated the mosaic pieces of jade and green light flashed across the glass table.

"A single mask won't replace fifty castles," Sir Philip said.

"No, you are right. This mask will only get a couple of million in the right market. But what if I place another one beside it?" Mr. Frost said.

Mr. Frost leaned over into the chest and pulled out another mask made of solid gold. He carefully set it next to the jade mask and sunrays danced across its surface, mixing with the green jade and creating an exotic light show on the glass table.

"Mr. Frost, you have yet to stimulate my imagination. I enjoyed the dive, but I will call the seaplane to pick me up before dark and I will return to Belize City to fly back to London. If I didn't have business in Miami, I would say you have wasted my time, dear sir," he said, standing up and preparing to leave for his cabin.

"Please sit down," Mr. Frost said.

Sir Philip looked at him, shrugged his shoulders, and sat back down. He rubbed the perspiration on his forehead and adjusted his reading glasses, which had slid down on his nose.

Mr. Frost reached into the box and pulled out an old book the size of a large photo album. It had a crude binding that was unidentifiable to Sir Philip Patterson, who was a London entrepreneur and dealer in underworld antiquities. Sir Philip carefully turned the pages until he came to a large diagram. He couldn't recognize the language written on the pages or the many hieroglyphs.

"O.K. You've got my curiosity," Sir Philip said.

"Before last week, there were three codices known to exist belonging to the ancient Mayans. Those are tucked away in museums in Dresden, Paris, and Madrid. This is codex number four, and it was found in a cathedral in southern France. It belonged to the Society of Jesus, the Jesuits, who recognized it as a threat to their evangelization of the Mayans, but had the foresight not to destroy it. They loved books and manuscripts and felt that someday they could read it without emotion. They were right. However, one of my agents came across it, and with help from a couple of scholars, we've determined that the ancient glyphs tell the history of this region of the Mayan realm. We now know where every temple and tomb was built. There is also writing in the Quichè language from someone who was trying to interpret the Mayan glyphs. Then the rest of the writing is in

Castilian Spanish, again trying to interpret what the Quichè said it meant.

"This codex tells us where every city-state exists in the Yucatan, Belize, Guatemala, and Honduras. The Spanish invaders required the priests to tabulate names and places and then the governor appointed by Spain wrote a summary of all the documents that was placed in the codex. Each ruling family is listed and was later corroborated by Mayan scholars as the many stele and temples were discovered and chronicled in scholarly works. When I have all the codices, I will be able to cross-reference them and pinpoint the actual escape route of the Mayan kings as the Spaniards moved in from the north. When I have their exact route, I can locate where they hid the lost treasure of the Mayan kings. Its value is in the billions.

"Both the priests and the Quichè had before them the key to unlock the mystery of the ancient Mayans. For the first time, we can tie together their astronomy, their religion, their culture, and their language," Mr. Frost said and looked up finally taking his eyes off of the masterpiece. "This is the Mayan equivalent of the Rosetta Stone."

Sir Philip stood up and rubbed his chin. He took a drink from his glass and set it down.

"A jolly good story but like I said, I'm not interested. I have maps of lost Viking treasure in Scotland that will keep me busy for the next two years. My associate, Mike O'Neal, is heading up that enterprise. Maybe you should put your interest in the British Isles rather than a mosquito-infested jungle," Patterson said.

"O'Neal? I thought the Leprechaun was dead," Mr. Frost said and stood up to face Patterson.

"No, the Leprechaun is alive and well," Sir Philip replied. "He has expanded his business from Ireland to the Middle East to Australia."

"Sir Philip, I prefer to work alone instead of with a crime syndicate the size of the Leprechaun's," Mr. Frost answered.

"My dear Mr. Frost, we are not a crime syndicate. We are simply good businessmen who band together to keep a strong alliance to insure greater profits," Patterson replied.

"Well put, but I prefer the beauty of solitude that can only be found working alone. This offering to you was simply an act of courtesy," Mr. Frost said, knowing now he never should have made it.

"Courtesy, was it? I thought you might want access to my assets," he sneered. "I think we've chatted enough. Good bye, Mr. Frost," Patterson said indignantly and walked away.

When Patterson had gone below to his cabin, Mr. Frost summoned two of his brawny deck hands.

"Take Sir Philip to the marina deck. Slit his throat and dump him into the blue hole near any reef sharks you can find. Oh, and take off his clothes, watch, and anything that might give the sharks indigestion. You know—pull out any dentures or gold teeth that would make his skull identifiable. We wouldn't want to leave a trail or harm nature, would we?" Mr. Frost said and smiled.

He checked the time on the big clock that hung on the outside of the lounge. It read 4:00 p.m. He knew it was time. Mr. Frost walked toward the lounge and through a spacious room to a series of stairs that took him three floors below deck. At the end of the hall, he stopped and took off the soft cotton robe. He opened a closet door and took out a royal blue ski suit. He quickly put it on, pulling all the zippers tight. Then he slipped on insulated boots, gloves, and a cotton beanie for his head.

As he opened a door at the end of the hall, a blast of cold air hit him in the face and he shivered. He inhaled the cold air and blew out a large breath. He fixed a pair of ski goggles over his eyes and sat down inside the small chamber. With his thickly padded gloves he reached out and pushed a large, black button that immediately turned on the Bose stereo built into the wall of the environmental chamber. The classical music of Schubert began to play and Frost leaned back in the plastic chair and closed his eyes. The big red digital letters of the clock on the wall were counting down from 120 minutes. The digital thermometer read 45 degrees Fahrenheit. This was the moment he had waited for all day.

At Camp Itzam Na, Chris had gathered gear along with the people who were to carry it, meaning Heather, R.O., and Natalie, and bid goodbye to Dr. North, Dr. Craven, and R.O.'s new friend Katelynn. They lowered themselves through a hatch in the flooring to reach the rainforest trolley system. Within minutes, they were zooming through the third-tier canopy toward the resort that was reserved for people who studied birds.

As they neared the end of the trolley system, Chris pulled the lever and was instantly released and dropped quickly to the platform that looked like their tree house back in North Texas. Soon all four teens were there and were unfastening their harnesses. R.O. was the first off the platform and was running toward the bungalow where he expected to find his parents, Jack and Mavis MacGregor. Instead when he reached the cabin he found a note that read:

Gone on a nature hike. We have dinner tonight with the archeology team, the birders, and some people from the government. Be there at 6:00 sharp, clean and pressed. —Mom

"Back to the cabins. It's 4:30 now. We've got time for a short nap and to clean-up," Chris said.

"No, that's barely enough time to shower and do my hair," Heather barked.

"You'll survive," R.O. said and walked toward his cabin where he bunked with Chris.

As Mr. Frost began to cool down, his skin tightened and his blood vessels constricted, relieving him of the pain he suffered when his skin got too warm. His doctors had never figured out how he had contracted such an awful disease, but Mr. Frost had managed to live with it. His billionaire status provided him with the resources to buy the portable cooling units he carried with him all over the world. The tropics were especially harsh on his condition because of the heat, but it was the tropics that Mr. Frost loved so much. His passion for collecting artifacts from ancient civilizations was what drove him to put himself in danger more often than a sane man would.

He shifted the beanie on his head as he reached the optimum temperature for his skin disease. Mr. Frost endured the extreme cold for two hours a day, because he knew the pain of his skin flaking off his body and the fluids leaking out, which would happen if he did not spend time in the cold, was even more painful and life threatening. He would spend the hours of frigid solitude thinking about the sport he loved more than any other—golf. In his mind, he would play the great golf courses of the world. Having mastered a hole-in-one twice, Mr. Frost knew the passion of victory. His golfing partners also knew that he must win the match or their lives would be at risk. Losing was not in his vocabulary.

Frost knew that this venture into the Yucatan of Mexico and the highlands of Belize was the greatest risk he had ever taken. But the millions of dollars in gold he held in his own private bank in Switzerland were not enough. He wanted more. Owning something that no other man could have was the elixir that stimulated all the nerves in his body. If his plan worked, he would be the greatest collector in the world. That was his reason for living.

One hundred miles away in Belize City, a middle-aged man with a full gray beard stepped off a small commuter aircraft and adjusted his straw hat.

"What a ride!" Mickey Banister said out loud. "Almost as good as the Texas Giant."

"What's that?" said a lady who had sat next to him during the turbulent ride.

"Just about the best darn wooden roller coaster in the world, madam," Banister replied.

"And where would I find this Texas Giant?" she said smiling.

"Six Flags Over Texas," Banister replied as he walked away toward the airport terminal.

He looked around the crowd of waiting families and business associates and noticed a man holding a card that read "Dead Shot 44." He laughed and knew that someone in FBI headquarters had tipped this guy off to the story of how he got the name in Alaska. Mickey Banister, FBI, walked over to the tall, bald man with the sign who was dressed in a white, casual shirt and pants with brown leather sandals. His holstered gun was on his belt.

"I'm Banister," he said.

"Mr. Banister, it's good to meet you. I'm Inspector Don Proctor, Belize National Police," the man said. "I've been instructed to greet you and take you to your hotel. Afterward we have a meeting with Chief Inspector Lidia at the local police headquarters about the looting."

"Excellent," Banister said and retrieved his bag from the baggage cart that had driven from the plane to the small terminal.

The short ride to the hotel took only five minutes and was filled with small talk about the weather. Ten minutes after checking in and dropping his bag in his room, Banister was back in the police car with Proctor, making small talk about crimes and people—something that Mickey hated to do. It was the part of the job that he disliked the most. But the excitement of solving the mystery of a crime was what had kept him in the Bureau when he was supposed to have retired after he wrapped up the case in Alaska four months earlier.

Arriving back in the peaceful city of Amarillo, Texas, Mickey could only stand a month of retirement before his lovely wife Jane convinced him that he was too young to retire and that five more years in the FBI would be good for him. So with only two days left before his retirement would be official, Mickey called Bureau headquarters and notified them of his desire to stay active. The director was more than pleased to hear the news, because Special Agent Banister had made the news and reinforced a good image for the Bureau after their success in Alaska. Mickey Banister had been labeled a real American hero.

The small Toyota-sedan police car stopped in front of the police headquarters and Banister followed Inspector Proctor inside. Turning down a long hall, both were escorted to a private room where a man and a woman had been waiting for them. The man rose and greeted them.

"Good afternoon, Special Agent," the older man said. He wore the rank of a senior officer on the epaulet of his khaki uniform-shirt and had several ribbons of valor and service on his chest. Banister could immediately recognize that he was a man of authority.

"Good afternoon," Mickey replied as he shook his hand.

"Please have a seat," the man said. "I'm Chief Inspector Dan Lidia, and this is Dr. Kim Spencer, director of antiquities."

"It's a pleasure, Inspector, Dr. Spencer," Mickey said. He took off his Panama hat and laid it on the table, noticing Spencer's flaming red hair.

"Special Agent Banister, we have a great problem," Lidia said. "Did Inspector Proctor fill you in?"

"No, but that's what I'm here for," Banister replied and opened a warm Dr. Pepper that was on the tray in the middle of the table.

"Can I get you a cold one, Mr. Banister?" Proctor asked.

"No, I prefer Dr. Peppers warm," he replied.

"Over the last sixteen months, looting has increased by 400 percent in the undeveloped pyramids and city ruins across the Mayan country from Mexico to Honduras," Dr. Spencer said.

"Do you know who's behind it?" Banister asked and took a drink of the soda.

"No, we haven't a clue. It has to be a large, organized force because the looters are well equipped and armed. They've killed seventeen guards who interfered with their looting or were stationed nearby where they were digging," Proctor said. "They've held landowners at gun point for days until their dig was completed."

"We also know that they have access to satellite maps that reveal some of the ancient ruins deep in the rainforest that even our specialists haven't been able to locate," she said. "It's like someone was guiding them to each new dig. It's mind-boggling. By the time we arrive, days after they have dug deep into the hidden temples, they are long gone and the trail is cold," Spencer said, getting up from her chair and pacing around.

"So how does that pertain to the FBI and the security of the United States?" Banister asked pointedly.

"We need someone who can unravel the mystery of the illegal antiquities trade, and Washington said you were our man," Lidia said.

"We're not inept or ignorant, Special Agent. We just need someone from the outside to look at the facts and maybe notice something that we've missed," Proctor said, as he adjusted his seating in his chair so his GLOCK 23 .40 caliber pistol was free from the right side of the chair—a habit that all lawmen learn.

"I see. My Spanish is a little rusty, but I do know a little about ancient artifacts. Archeology was my minor in college, and I pick up something now and then from a legal dealer. I've also worked a few cases involving artifact smugglers," Banister responded.

"Good, then we have you on board," Lidia said.

"Certainly. I needed a tropical vacation and this is as good as any," Banister laughed. "Glad to be of service, Chief Inspector Lidia. I mean Lidee."

"Inspector Proctor and Dr. Spencer will be your contacts and liaison," Lidia said rising from his chair. "Don't worry. Everyone says it wrong the first time."

"I will be in the north for a few days before I can join you. We have a drug problem along the border with Mexico,"

Proctor said. "If you should need me, Dr. Spencer has my cell phone number."

Banister shook hands with Chief Inspector Lidia and Inspector Proctor and then followed Dr. Spencer from the room and out to her SUV.

On the *Calakmul Queen,* Ron Frost was finishing his daily cooling session as treatment for his skin disease. He shivered as his skin tingled when it met the warm tropical air. He shed the heavy ski suit, mittens, and cap quickly so he wouldn't drive up his body heat, and walked to his office next to the large lounge on the main deck. As he opened up his computer, he noticed an emergency-flashing icon and clicked on it. His e-mail opened up and he read the encrypted note:

Vienna is a beautiful city and we are bringing you a souvenir.

London was cold and windy, but Paris opened her arms to us.

Mr. Frost smiled. He knew that his men had secured the artifacts in Vienna, and that the Mayan codex in Paris had been taken as well. London apparently had been a bust, but he knew he still needed to get the mask and the crystal skull from the British Museum. He searched through his mail and finally turned it off. Mr. Frost had been waiting for word from Madrid, the home of the other Mayan codex. He checked his watch and calculated that it was near midnight in Madrid. There was still enough time that he could have the other codex by morning. The only one left was in Dresden, Germany.

Getting up from his net chair, which breathed and kept him cool, he walked to the end of the lounge and looked around at the turquoise Caribbean Sea. What a beautiful place—it angered him that he couldn't enjoy it more. He heard steps behind him.

"Mr. Frost, your guest is here," the deck hand declared.

5

Chicken of the Tree

Natalie and Heather wandered down the path between two cleaned and scrubbed Mayan temples in the middle of the resort where they were staying. Built by a land owner who wanted to protect the ruins of the ancient civilization at Xnaheb in southern Belize, the resort was also a way to make a handsome income from tourists. Archeologists and government officials had argued about the development, but the owner had his rights; he was a fifth-generation owner whose grandfather had cleaned out the temples and buildings by hand, long before the scientists had taken interest in them. The owner had named the resort Jade Sky after a king of Quiriqua, an ancient city to the south, who had lived and fought for the land a thousand years ago.

As the two girls stepped inside their bungalow, they immediately felt the relief provided by the small air conditioning unit they shared with an adjacent set of rooms.

"I'm wiped," Heather said and fell backwards on the bed.

"Well, don't you think a bath will help, before you get all of the jungle on your sheets," Natalie said.

"You're right. How gross. That was dumb of me," Heather said and jumped up quickly.

Next door, Chris was already in the shower as R.O. opened his suitcase and pulled out his latest invention. Only Ryan would be able to recognize what it was or did, and the only obvious thing about it was the electrical cord coming from the white base. R.O. tinkered with the item, which looked like a blender, for a while until Chris finished his shower. Though he loved to make things by hand, R.O. was beginning to lose his fondness for it, because of the many adventures with his family. There just wasn't enough free time to dedicate to it. So he had decided to collect as many parts as he could, so that when the time came, he could assemble a new invention.

"Water pressure is low, so I would hurry in case the hot water runs out," Chris said as he toweled off. "Be careful with the stitches on your ear. Dr. Craven said a little water wouldn't hurt it."

"I will," R.O. said and winced as he reached up and touched his ear.

Time passed quickly and six o'clock arrived. Natalie and Heather knocked on their door just as Chris was strapping on his hiking sandals. The four teens walked through the Mayan resort complex until they came to the main dining room. They could hear the buzz of dozens of conversations, growing louder as they approached. The dining room was just one big banquet hall that looked like it belonged in the jungle, decorated with earth tones and fabrics that fit the culture of Belize.

"There sure are a lot of old people here," R.O. said.

"Those are probably the retired folks who like to watch birds," Natalie said.

"Birders," Chris said.

"Yes, I know what they call themselves," Natalie replied.

"There's Dad," Heather said and started walking in his direction.

As Heather approached, Jack MacGregor got a glimpse of his daughter and turned to hug her.

"Hey Dad," she said.

"Hey back. Did y'all have a good time on your tour this afternoon?" Jack asked as Natalie walked up to them.

"Yeah, sure. It was great," Heather said a little too quickly.

"That sounded odd. Anything exciting happen that I need to know about?" Jack asked as he turned to greet Natalie.

"Not a thing," came Chris' voice from behind. "Heather bumped her head. Want to take a look?" he said to Jack.

Heather found the spot and closed her eyes as Jack examined it.

"You did get a nasty bump. How do you feel?" Jack asked, looking her straight in the eyes.

"What's all the fuss?" Mavis MacGregor said as she appeared through the crowd.

"Heather bumped her head," R.O. said to his Mom, as Chris put his hand on his shoulder and squeezed.

"Hey, that hurts," R.O. said, forcing Chris to let go. R.O. stepped back, but not before Mavis caught a glimpse of the nasty tear on his ear.

"My mother the queen!" she exclaimed. "What on earth happened to that ear? It looks awful. Jack! Jack, look at your son's ear," Mavis said and spun around to face Chris.

"Your turn," she said firmly and looked him in the eyes.

"He was playing with a cat and it snagged him on the ear," Chris said with a sober face. "Dr. Craven at Camp Itzam Na stitched it up. It looks great now, don't you think?"

Heather had to turn around to avoid showing her face, trying to hide her laughter.

"A cat was it? Me own mum's giant tabby wouldn't leave a wound that big," Mavis fired back in her British accent.

"What kind of cat?" Jack asked calmly.

"A female jaguar," Chris said quickly.

"And why the emphasis on female, son?" Jack asked firmly, as if in an interrogation.

"Oops, did you slip up," Natalie whispered to Chris, who gave her a nasty look in return.

"Because I was playing with the cub and when the mother

jaguar came home, I got scared and stuffed the cub in my pack and took off on the canopy trolley," R.O. said.

"Jack, it's time for coffee. Sweetie," she said, turning to Heather. "Find me a cup and you know how to doctor it up. And quick!" Mavis exclaimed. "Why do I feel like there is more to this story? Don't things come in threes? You know that old American saying or something. And it seems the MacGregor kids always have threes."

"Or fours," piped in Natalie.

"Please, don't remind me," Mavis said.

"Well, Heather got hit in the head from a rock and was knocked out when we fell down the chute inside the pyramid, and if it hadn't been for Chris she would have drowned in the underground lake," R.O. said without taking a breath.

"Ryan!" Jack said firmly. "Past experience tells me that this isn't a tall tale but something that really did happen," Jack said.

"Here's a table over here for six. Shouldn't we sit down?" Natalie said trying to help distract Heather's parents.

"Good idea, Natalie. Were you involved in all of this, too?" Mavis said as she took the coffee from Heather.

"Yes. And Chris was our hero again. He is just amazing, Dr. MacGregor," Natalie said.

"I told you, it's Mavis," Mavis corrected her.

"Yes, Ma'm," Natalie replied.

"This must be all the MacGregors," boomed the voice of Dr. David North, chief archaeologist of Camp Itzam Na.

"Yes, I'm Jack MacGregor," Jack said and started to stand.

"Don't get up Dr. MacGregor. I met all of the kids today on our floating camp on top of the rainforest," North said.

"How did you get up there?" Mavis asked quickly, still examining the wound on R.O.'s ear.

"They were our first guests actually," Dr. North said.

"That's a nasty cut. Did you tell your mother about the giant jaguar?" Katelynn Komarovski said, as she stepped from behind Dr. North.

R.O. sat up straight and pulled away from his mother.

"Hi R.O.," Katelynn said.

"Hi Katelynn," R.O. replied.

Mavis noticed the energy pass between the two thirteen-year-olds and worked to hide her smile.

"How's the ear?" Katelynn asked. All other conversation halted to hear the two interact.

"No problem. I've had cuts before," R.O replied in a manly fashion.

"But not one that almost took your head off," Heather observed, receiving a quick glare from R.O.

"We'll hear the rest of the story later," Jack said trying to break up the overbearing crowd.

"I'm starved," Heather was first to say followed by Natalie.

Chris didn't speak but just followed the girls to the buffet.

"I had our camp doctor, Dr. Craven, take a look at Heather's head injury. Dr. Craven said she might have gotten a small concussion because she did lose consciousness for a time," Dr. North said.

"Heather was knocked out? Oh my word!" Mavis said and turned toward Heather, who had just left for the buffet.

"Did they tell you how it happened?" Jack asked quietly.

"Yes, they were inside temple number fourteen being pursued by looters when the inside shaft gave way. Their combined weight and 1,200 years of aging was too much for the old sacrificial chute," Dr. North said.

"Looters! This trip is not starting out so well," Mavis whispered and took another drink of her coffee.

"When do they ever?" Jack replied and patted her hand that was resting on the table.

"I saw the tear in the young guy's ear. You folks must live daring lives," Dr. North said and chuckled.

"That we do," Jack replied and looked at Mavis.

"Dr. Craven said to keep an eye on her for dizziness or not walking straight, you know, normal behavior that goes off pattern. She's a competent ER doc or I wouldn't have hired her for this mission," Dr. North said.

"I'm sure she is," Mavis replied, feeling more assured.

"Come and see us anytime on the top of the rainforest," Dr. North said and got up to leave.

"We'll do that. I'm sure the kids loved it. Thank you," Mavis said.

"Yes, and those younger ones hit it off well," Dr. North said.

"This would be his first female friend. Should be interesting to watch," Mavis said.

Dr. North turned and walked away as Mavis and Jack just looked at each other in silent surprise.

"Not much to say, is there?" Jack spoke first.

"No. We've done all of this before. We should just expect that when our kids go out on their own they will be exploring the world and will do things that they shouldn't do. Just poor judgment," Mavis said.

"Not poor judgment, just ignorance to the consequences," Jack replied.

"Who are you calling ignorant?" R.O. said from behind them, as he and Katelynn pulled up chairs and began eating.

"What'd you find to eat, honey?" Mavis asked him.

"Lots of fried chicken strips," Katelynn said.

"Those aren't fried chicken strips," Natalie said as she walked up. "It's iguana."

"Oh yuk!" R. O. said first.

"Yup, pure dee chicken of the tree," Natalie replied.

"It does taste a little like chicken. I've had it lots of times," Katelynn replied as she took a tiny bite. "Put some gravy on it and see if you like it."

Heather walked up with a plate full of food and sat down. She quickly put the fried iguana in her mouth and started chewing.

"Hmmm. Those are great chicken strips," she said and everyone started laughing.

"O.K. What's going on? Do I have something hanging out of my nose? Or am I bleeding from my scalp again?" Heather demanded.

"No, no, sweetie, you aren't bleeding," Mavis said in an apologetic tone. "It's just we were talking about food when you walked up and . . ."

"Noticed you were chowing down on the fried reptile," R.O. interrupted quickly.

"Fried reptile? What fried reptile?" Heather asked still eating the iguana. "This is fried chicken. I wouldn't eat reptile. That's *disgusting*."

"News flash, little sister," Chris said as he sat down next to her. "That's fried iguana you have in your mouth."

Heather gasped and nearly sucked the iguana down her windpipe, choking. As her gag reflex started, she threw up the chewed and ingested iguana on her plate and the surrounding table, followed by all the water and soda she drank, along with the crackers she had eaten in her room.

"Oh gross," R.O. cried out, jumping back from the vomit splatter that was everywhere.

Heather heaved again from the reflex and more food came up; then she started dry heaving. Mavis moved quickly behind her to be ready in case she gagged and couldn't breathe. She reached out to pull Heather's hair away from her face when Mavis accidentally touched the bump on her head.

"Ouch!" Heather yelled and had another dry heave.

"Natalie, go get some wet towels, please," Mavis said.

But before Natalie could get up from the table, two wait staff appeared with damp cloths for Heather and the table. In just a couple of minutes, everything was cleaned up and Heather was leaning back in her chair with a wash cloth on her forehead.

"Sweets, I've ordered some plain old chicken noodle soup to calm your stomach," Mavis said.

"Are you sure it's real chicken?" Heather asked quietly.

"Yes, I told them I wanted chicken not iguana," Mavis replied. "Isn't it *pollo* in Spanish?"

"That's right," Natalie replied.

"Then that's what I ordered," Mavis said.

"Thanks, Mom. You're the best. I have a headache now," Heather replied.

"That was a nasty bump you got. It's to be expected," Mavis said.

"Yeah, all I remember was sliding down the rocky chute inside the temple and then something hit me in the head. I don't even remember free falling forty feet into the cenote," Heather said.

"Forty feet? It's amazing you didn't get hurt worse," Mavis said, trying to stay calm.

"Ryan was below all of us and fell into the water first and swam away from the rock slide. Then it took us an hour to climb back out, but we ended up in a second pyramid. We found a passageway from the king's chambers to an escape tunnel. I can't remember where it was. My head was pounding by then," Heather said and took the cloth off her face.

"So how did you get to Camp Itzam Na?" Mavis asked, still curious.

"That was easy. We were just pulled up a rope and suddenly we were inside. It's really cool. Can we stop talking now?" Heather asked as soup and fresh bread were delivered to the table.

"Sure, honey. You need to eat," Mavis said and turned to the other youth who had moved one table away. "Getting enough to eat?"

"Yeah, Mom. The stew is really good," R.O. was the first to speak up.

"And no, we don't want to know what's in the stew," Natalie spoke before Mavis could take a breath.

"Honey, I got an email from Australia when I checked a few moments ago and Ryan . . ." Jack said loudly so R.O.

could hear him. "You've got a message from Drew you need to respond to."

"Thanks, Dad," R.O. said.

"Are we going to Australia next?" Natalie asked and took a bite of a hard roll. It was her third roll already.

"I don't know, yet," Jack replied and took a drink of tea.

"Who's in Australia, Dad?" Chris asked.

"Dr. Harold Shank. You remember him. He's the United Nations cultural arbitrator," Jack said and ate a piece of fried iguana.

"What's that mean?" Natalie asked.

"He's sent wherever two cultures clash and their differences can't be resolved," Jack replied.

"What's that got to do with you?" Chris asked his zoologist father.

"Yes, I would like to know that, too," Mavis said, sipping on her fourth cup coffee.

"There are new disagreements with the aboriginal people in Australia and the Maori in New Zealand, so Dr. Shank was sent to work as an arbitrator with both governments," Jack replied and drank more tea. "The report he sent said there was some discussion about habitat encroachment, gemstone mining, and a lot more. I haven't read it all yet."

"Is that where we're going after we leave Belize?" Natalie asked.

"Maybe, I like Dr. Shank. He's a good man and I would like to help out. It will give me a chance to include Australia's declining marsupial population in my book," Jack said. "But I've received a note from the Prime Minister of Rwanda concerning some new gorilla poaching problems in neighboring Congo. We'll just have to wait and see where we go next, but we'll definitely go to both."

"Excellent," Mavis said loudly. "Isn't Dr. Shank's wife named Sally?"

"Yes, I believe she is," Jack said.

"I just loved her when we met in New York at the U.N.

dinner a year ago in May, I think it was. We got off smashingly," Mavis said throwing in one of her favorite British expressions. "My months are beginning to run together. So if I am counting correctly it's Australia, New Zealand, Rwanda, and then back to England to see Pop and me Mum."

"But what about Russia, the Amazon, and India?" Chris asked.

"I don't know yet. We'll see," Jack said and ate another "chicken strip."

6

Codex of Madrid

The Volvo drove through the dark streets of the central district of Madrid on the Paseo de San Francisco and turned east down an alley, one block from the Calle de Maria de Molina and just three blocks from the Museo de América. It was four past midnight. The car traveled about three hundred feet until it reached a wrought-iron fence about ten feet tall and topped with razor wire. Kiley, a young, 5′4″ woman with flaming red hair and Bill, a tall, thin man with a balding head, got out of the car, opened the trunk, and lifted out a camouflage net big enough to cover the car. Even in the darkness, Kiley's red hair could be seen sticking out from under the black knit cap. Once the car was secured, the man lifted a large duffle from the back seat and unfolded it completely. They each grabbed a fully automatic 9mm Mini-Uzi, a .40 caliber Walther P99AS pistol, a utility belt full of gear they would need, and a knit mask for their faces. Kiley pulled a small pneumatic rifle with a stainless-steel spear sticking out of the barrel with a nylon cord in a reel attached to it out of the trunk. She clamped it to her utility belt so she wouldn't drop it. Bill pulled out a large piece of folded material, unrolling it and revealing a large balloon.

Bill pulled a tube from the floor of the back seat and connected it to the balloon while Kiley pushed a button under the leather seat. Instantly a quiet compressor turned on and helium began to flow into the balloon, inflating quickly. In just about a minute the balloon was floating over the car in the dark alley and Bill and Kiley grabbed on and hung on tightly to it. Soon the balloon began to lift them off the ground. They held tightly on to the open window of the car until they couldn't any longer.

They let go and the compressor tube broke free from the balloon. It sealed shut automatically and shot up quickly as they hung from ropes attached to its side. Ten feet, twenty feet, thirty feet, and then they cleared the top of the building to the east. The anticipated gust of wind from the east blew the balloon toward the adjacent street four hundred feet away. They were now seventy feet in the air and passing over the Museo de America. Kiley reached down to her side and pointed the pneumatic rifle toward one of the massive medieval turrets on top of the building. Aiming quickly, she pulled the trigger and the arrow shot through the air and hit the wood tower perfectly. She then began to reel them in toward the top of the building.

"We're coming down too fast," Kiley Spencer said.

"No. Just right," Bill Thompson replied, a forty-year veteran of such clandestine activities.

Two minutes passed before they were standing firmly on the roof of one of Spain's most famous museums of antiquities.

Bill took a sharp knife and stabbed the balloon and the remaining helium rushed out. Both knew that their only escape now was through the inside of the museum. There was no turning back.

They walked carefully across the roof until they reached the domed skylight located over the central atrium of the museum. Bill opened his pack and pulled out a vacuum-cup device. He pressed it to the glass portion of the skylight and pulled on the metal tab in the middle. An instantly created vacuum held it in place. Kiley started cutting a circle around it. In seconds, the piece of glass was cut and removed. Bill reached inside and flipped the latch that locked the skylight window. Soon it was propped up and both were standing on a small catwalk that wrapped around the ceiling on the inside of the museum's massive rotunda.

"Pretty slick, Bill. Motion detectors, dogs, concertina wire, electric fence, and we just go up and over it in five minutes. I'm impressed. You really know how to show a girl a good time," Kiley whispered and smiled at him.

"Not so bad for someone thirty years your senior," Bill replied and pulled down his knit mask. "Don't forget there're cameras inside."

"With you, Bill, age doesn't matter a bit," she said with a wink before pulling down her mask.

"O.K., let's see how good we really are," Bill replied. He tied a rope across the railing of the catwalk and climbed over.

Connecting his rappelling belt to the rope, he lowered himself to the main floor of the museum. Once on the tiled floor, he waved for Kiley and soon she was standing next to him.

"The auxiliary power box should be located over there next to the statue of Columbus. The rotunda was originally the entrance to the building. Then a new section was added on after World War II. The building is now on two separate power grids," Bill said as he walked forward.

"What about motion sensors?" Kiley asked.

"After I robbed this place back in '86, they installed sensors with laser beams but they only put them on the halls next to the exits. They didn't think that anyone would come through the antique glass dome. The guards sit in a little room in the basement watching their monitors," Bill said.

"Antique? Oh my," Kiley said as she looked up. "We cut a hole right through the face of St. Mary. We're going to Hell for sure, Bill!"

"My point exactly. Let's get moving. The cameras cycle through every ten minutes. It's now 12:15 and we'll be right behind each cycle," Bill replied.

The two thieves walked purposefully through the main halls of the museum until they reached a large glass case that held a miniature wooden ship.

"First case to the right of the ship. There it is," Bill said.

Kiley walked over to the glass case and shined her small flashlight down on the *Codex of Madrid,* one of three known Mayan manuscripts in existence.

"Isn't she a masterpiece? What my sister Kim would give to be here to see this," Kiley said and began feeling around the case for alarm wires.

"Don't waste your time. The wire is placed in the glass. Break any part of the glass or even lean on it too hard and the alarm goes off," Bill replied.

"What do we do now?" Kiley asked.

"Watch and you'll see," he replied and crawled under the case.

He felt along its legs until he found the spot where one leg had been repaired after the alarm wire had been fed through the leg to the glass connector. Taking out one of his small tools, he began to carve into the leg until he could see the blue and red wires running vertically.

"Hand me my pack," Bill said softly.

Kiley passed him the pack and he pulled out a small plastic box with wires hanging out two sides. Taking the red wire from the box, he connected it to the red wire in the table leg. He then did the same for the blue wire. He pulled out another small box that had a battery in it and he connected the white wire to the bare copper wire running next to the blue and red ones in the leg.

"That last one grounded it. Some of these alarms will still go off—even if you have bypassed the circuit—if they aren't grounded," Bill declared and crawled out from under the case.

He stood up and took out a knife from his belt. With the

steel butt, he came crashing down on the glass with all of his might. The glass case shattered into thousands of pieces and Kiley jumped back.

"Wow," she said as Bill stepped forward and picked up the *Codex of Madrid* carefully, dusting off the broken glass with his gloved hand.

"Hand me the transport case," Bill said.

Kiley reached into her pack and pulled out a waterproof, rubber-lined case that fit the manuscript perfectly. She unrolled it.

"One would think you had this specially made for the Codex," Kiley said.

"I did, but the maker hasn't a clue who paid him to make it. If he had, I would have had to eliminate him," Bill replied calmly.

"Remind me not to cross you, Bill," Kiley said cautiously.

"You have no worries. I never kill women," Bill said.

"That's good to know," Kiley replied.

"I pay others to do that for me," Bill said and laughed.

He checked his OMEGA watch and looked up.

"We've got thirteen minutes before the bypass fails and the alarms go off. Follow me," Bill said.

The two thieves strode through the massive halls that were crammed with art and statues until they reached an office area.

"We can leave through the employees' entrance," Bill said. "We've got four minutes before the cameras catch up with us."

Kiley followed quickly until they had run through a maze of offices and stopped at the security entrance. Bill took out a card-key that was attached to an electronic cipher box. He swiped the card and held it there until the cipher box found the random code and flipped the switch to open the door. They walked through the door and Bill stopped at the second security station, walked inside, and flipped the alarm to the off position.

"They always want to keep you out, but never think about keeping you in," Bill said. "Leave your rifle. It's clean and untraceable."

Kiley dropped hers next to Bill's on a secretary's desk.

Once out the door, in unison, they pulled off their masks and dropped them to the ground along with their knit caps. They then walked down the big steps to the employee parking lot and across the street to a small cantina that was going strong with customers and music.

"Over here," Bill said as Kiley followed him to the motorcycle rack.

Bill stepped across a black Yamaha motorcycle, put in a key, and fired it up. Kiley strapped the codex in its protective case across her back and slid onto the saddle behind him. Bill looked at his watch.

"Ten seconds," Bill said and sped away from the cantina with the massive museum looming across the street.

They moved quickly through several intersections and had traveled one mile, when the alarms of the Museo de América kicked on and lights, bells, and whistles went off in unison. The sleepy night watchman ran through the great halls looking for anything that could have set it off until he came to the smashed case of the *Codex of Madrid.* He scratched his head and wondered why anyone would want the old manuscript with cases of diamonds and emeralds laying alongside it. He shrugged his shoulders.

Bill and Kiley reached the edge of Madrid in less than an hour. It was nearly 1:30 A.M. Bill drove the motorcycle next to a black Mercedes SUV and a Porsche Boxster S. Kiley got off the motorcycle and put the codex into the Mercedes. Bill put their packs and utility belts inside the Porsche. He put on a pair of glasses with clear lenses and no prescription. On any other day, he would be mistaken for an accountant or insurance executive. But tonight he was the famed *Gato Amarillo de Europa,* the yellow cat of Europe, as the European papers had called him through the years.

He walked over to the motorcycle and unscrewed the gas cap. He then set a two foot fuse and draped it from inside the gasoline down to the outside of the tank. He took out a lighter and lit the fuse.

"We have about ninety seconds before it blows," he said.

"What about the first car?" Kiley said.

"It blew fifteen minutes ago," Bill smiled.

"You leave nothing to chance, do you?" Kiley said.

"No I don't. Now what about . . ."

"Your money? I just texted my buyer and his reply is right here," she held up the cell phone for Bill to see.

Bill then dialed up his bank account in Switzerland and verified that $2 million had been deposited, less than five minutes before.

"We're done," Bill replied.

Kiley stepped over close to him and gave him a friendly kiss.

"Thanks, Bill," she said as she stepped back.

"Anytime, kiddo," he replied.

Both hopped into their cars and sped away just as the gas tank caught on fire and the motorcycle exploded into thousands of pieces.

The next morning Special Agent Mickey Banister, FBI, met the director of antiquities, Kim Spencer, in the lobby of his small hotel in Belize. Stretching after sleeping on a mattress that was overstuffed and too soft, Banister munched on a hard roll he had stashed in his pocket from dinner the night before. Not one for big breakfasts, he preferred two big meals a day.

"How was your breakfast, Mr. Banister?" Spencer asked as she strode up, noticing the roll in his hand.

"For a day-old roll, it's not bad," Banister replied and took another bite. "Where are we off to?"

"I have a list of dig sites I want to take you to," she replied.

"I'm ready when you are," Banister said.

"Let's go into the gift shop first," Spencer said and took

off in a fast walk, which made Banister happy because he hated to walk slowly. He always said that tourists or lazy folks were the ones who walk too slowly.

Spencer stopped suddenly in front of the men's clothing racks and one of her silver, hoop earrings spun around and tangled in her beautiful red hair. With a flip of her right hand it fell into place.

"Agent Banister, I am not being critical of your appearance but here in the tropics men wear these kinds of shirts," she said and pointed to a rack in front of her.

She reached up and grabbed a cream colored shirt that buttoned down the front and was made to hang on the outside of the pants. Then she picked up a khaki-colored pair of pants.

"Will these fit?" she asked Banister.

"Sure will," he answered as he looked at the tag.

She grabbed four more shirts and matching pants.

"See those sandals over there? Find a comfortable pair that straps across the heel," she said.

Mickey walked over to the shoe rack and quickly found a brown pair with firm soles. He then reached down two shelves and picked up a pair of canvas "jungle" boots.

"I think I like these better," Mickey said to himself.

"Now go put one of these on and I'll meet you in the car," Spencer smiled, handing him the clothes, and walked away.

"Yes, ma'am," Banister replied, feeling like he should salute.

After changing clothes and just before entering the lobby, Banister finally got his CZ 75 9mm fixed into the belt holster under the blousy shirt. The pistol had arrived via a courier at six that morning. When he opened the box and handled the new pistol, he loaded the clip and felt the nice balance. He felt secure again. He would miss not having his Ruger Super Redhawk .44 Magnum, but this wasn't Alaska, and the CZ 75 would work just fine. After all the Czech-made pistol was the weapon of choice of his old enemies, the Soviet KGB.

When Mickey stepped into Kim's four-wheel-drive vehicle, she noticed the tip of the holster as he put on his seatbelt.

"I won't ask where you got that, but I'm glad you carry one," she said and smiled.

"Got one what?" Mickey said and grinned.

"The first stop is about an hour away. From there we go up into the mountains about two hours. In all, we've got six stops, and we'll be back here around dinner time," Spencer said.

"I wouldn't want to miss dinner," Mickey said. "So, you're not from around here. How does an East Texan get a cushy job as director of antiquities in Belize?"

"East Texas, you are so good, Special Agent Banister," she said.

"Call me Mickey," he replied.

"O.K. Mickey, not East Texas but Houston," she replied, showing the twang in her voice. "My uncle is a native of Belize, who works in the government, and when they needed an archaeologist to help get their antiquities department back on its feet after several years of mismanagement and corruption, he gave me a call. My job is only temporary and then there will be several newly trained Belizean scholars to take over. In the meantime, I need to find out where all of the treasure of the Mayans is being taken."

"Treasure?" Mickey said.

"Yes, treasure—and lots of it," she replied.

"Tell me about it. My department just said to come down here and help out. I don't think they know what to do with me. I was scheduled to retire last week and changed my mind," Mickey said.

"Well I don't know you, so I can't say if that's good or bad," Spencer said.

"You wouldn't be related to Lady Diana Spencer, would you?" Mickey asked making a joke.

"As a matter of fact, I am. When she was alive, my mother did one of those genealogy things, you know what I mean. Well, she discovered we have a connection in England and one in Scotland. That's how my sister and I got the red hair," Spencer said.

"So you're not married?" Mickey asked.

"We'll not discuss that, thank you. And Spencer is my daddy's name," she said quickly.

"Where's your sister?" Mickey asked.

"She's in Belize, I think. She's a big SCUBA diver and hangs out with that crowd. She's an archaeologist, too," Kim said.

"That's interesting," Mickey said to keep the conversation going. As a Special Agent for the FBI, he was well trained in using casual conversation to serve as a type of interrogation to get as much information as possible.

"Yep, Daddy sent us both to U.T. in Austin for our degrees. He and Mama are pretty well set with all the oil drilling he did in East Texas."

"You have a very interesting family," Mickey replied.

"We sure do and we're proud of it," Spencer declared.

The casual chat eventually got around to the Mayan ruins being looted and how systematic the thefts had been.

"In the past, the lootings were random. A storm would blow in from the Caribbean and the mountainsides would get all muddy and some of the mudslides would uncover new temples. We often suspected temples were there, but did not have proof until after these storms. Tree roots have destroyed a lot of the stone buildings, and some start decaying from the inside out," Kim said.

"What caught your attention?" Mickey asked.

"Looters moved from either north to south or west to east in a pattern, uncovering ruins we didn't even know existed," she replied.

"So you think they have a map?" Mickey asked.

"Yes, I do. But where on earth would you get a map? None of the three Mayan codices in existence have maps. They are merely stories of culture and religion. Only experts can read them, and even then sometimes I think they guess at the meaning of some of the glyphs," Kim said.

"Logic says that someone has a map of some kind. Find the map, you find the kingpin behind the looting," Mickey said.

Mr. Frost walked out on the back deck of the *Calakmul Queen* with a crystal glass full of papaya juice in his hand. Having slept late after the telephone call from Madrid, he felt rested and ready for a full day. Taylor, a slender blonde of medium height and ship's officer, walked up to him with a telephone in hand.

"Frost here," he said.

"Guten morgen, Herr Frost. The business in Dresden was very good. I will ship you a souvenir today to your Miami office," the man said.

"Very good. Good day," Mr. Frost said and disconnected the call.

"The circle is complete," Mr. Frost said and drank down the papaya juice, throwing the crystal glass into the sea.

Mr. Frost turned to Taylor and spoke.

"Bring me my clubs and three dozen balls, I need to practice my nine iron," he said and turned toward the morning sun.

7

Stele Thirteen

Mavis MacGregor banged on the door of the cottage until Chris climbed out of bed, stumbled across backpacks and clothes, and opened the door.

"I'm coming. Hold on!" Chris yelled along the way.

"My, aren't we cheery this morning?" Mavis said with a smile.

"Good morning, Mom," Chris forced out, squinting his eyes as rays of sunshine slipped through the trees above them.

"You've got fifteen minutes to get dressed, properly geared up, and be at the dining room. The girls are already there waiting. Cheerio!" Mavis said to her barely awake son.

Chris closed the door, walked over to a sleeping R.O., and pulled off the sheet. He then grabbed him by the ankles and dragged him off the bed, where he fell on top of the clothes and boots he was wearing the day before.

"Ow! Hey, I'm still asleep!" R.O. yelled.

"Technically, no you aren't. We've got ten minutes to be at the dining hall. Mom just left," Chris said as he walked into the bathroom and turned on a shower with very low water pressure.

He took a quick shower and left the water running for R.O., who jumped right in.

"The water's cold," R.O. complained.

"No, it's cool. And use the soap. Your hair is all matted from yesterday," Chris said.

No answer came from the shower.

Fifteen minutes later, the two MacGregor brothers walked into the dining room to find only their family present. Natalie got up and walked up to Chris and kissed him on the cheek.

"Did you brush your teeth?" she whispered.

"What's a question like that have to do with anything?" Chris replied quickly.

"You'll know why later, if you didn't," she said and went back to her chair.

"Yeah, rocket scientist. Even I figured that one out," R.O. said as he walked by. "You guys are gross even in the mornings!"

"Good morning, gentlemen," Mavis said and smiled. "Glad you could join us. We have a full day ahead of us."

"Hey Dad," Chris said as he sat down.

"Hey back to you. We've got some great ruins to look at today," Jack said as he looked up from the tourist maps he had laid out on the table.

"Not more temples of doom?" Heather asked as she put a fork full of scrambled eggs into her mouth.

"Are you sure those aren't iguana eggs?" R.O. said and smiled.

"Stuff it, little brat, I mean *brother,*" Heather replied and took another big bite.

Mavis looked at both of them but decided to save the chastisement for a better moment, which she knew would come eventually.

"No temples of doom," Jack replied. "Just an ongoing dig east of here up into the mountains a ways."

"Good morning, MacGregors," boomed a voice from behind them. "Your four-wheeler is ready. Full tank of gas and two jerry cans on the back, also full. That should get you about two hundred miles today. More than enough to get you there and back," said the manager of the bungalows who appeared in front of them. "The kitchen also packed lunches for everyone and put in a case of bottled water."

"We're set then. Let's go," Jack said and got up.

Chris and R.O. tried to stuff down more bacon and eggs and each grabbed a couple of pieces of buttered toast as they ran to catch up with the others. Outside a faded-red Toyota Land Cruiser that had seen better days was waiting, as the resort staff crammed the last of the food behind the two back seats. The hard roof had been cut off and replaced with a canvas canopy. The two back seats had been welded to the floor, replacing the standard side seats. Foam padding was sticking out of the cracks in the upholstery. There were no seatbelts. The manager walked up to Jack and handed a satchel to him.

"Inside is a Smith & Wesson .40 caliber semiautomatic pistol. It's for any pesky snakes that might come your way. There are two extra clips. Be safe and if you see government people around, hide it inside the food containers. They don't think too kindly of weapons floating around among the tourists down here, but most tourists don't go where you guys are going," he said.

"Thank you. We'll be just fine," Mavis said and took the satchel from Jack, putting in on the floor of the Toyota between her feet.

Jack put the vehicle in gear and they headed down the road on what was supposed to have been their first Mayan adventure. Everyone was trying to forget about yesterday.

"Ryan, I mean R.O., how on earth did you get blue boots?" Mavis said as she turned around and noticed his boots for the first time. "Heather, you have one blue boot, too. How strange!"

"I don't know for sure, but when I fell out of the chute at the temple I came straight down, feet first, and went to the bottom of the lake. I guess it was about ten feet deep. I felt my feet stick into some gooey stuff and I had to swim hard to get out of it. I guess I swam up at an angle because the rocks were falling away from me. Later we noticed that the gooey stuff must have been something blue," R.O. explained. "Heather must have just got one foot in it."

Jack looked over his shoulder at the boots while he was trying to drive.

"It might be Maya Blue," he said.

"What's Maya Blue?" Natalie said from the back seat next to Chris.

"I'm not sure. It's not my territory. Let's ask one of the archaeologists when we get to the dig near Lubaantun," Jack said.

"That's a big dig," R.O. said and smiled.

"Don't say it!" Heather looked at him.

"What, that I'm a poet?" R.O. replied.

"This trip is getting so old with you," Heather said.

"Heather, when we stop, I'll trade seats with you. O.K.?" Mavis said.

"Thanks Mom. This is our eighth stop this year and well, you know," Heather said and brushed her hair back out of her face. She reached into her small gear bag and retrieved a yellow scrunchy and quickly pulled back her hair.

The old Land Cruiser hummed along for three hours as they followed a map, cross checking on the GPS device the resort manager loaned them. With each new fork in the road, the terrain got rougher and the road more pitted with holes. Jack could tell that the road was being used, despite its condition, by the number of fallen trees and rocks stacked beside it.

Heather was just about ready to call for a lunch break when they made a sharp turn in the rainforest road and a solid-rock stele appeared to their right, nestled between two trees. It must have been eight feet tall. Jack came to a stop and turned off the Toyota.

"My, my, my," Mavis said, getting out of the car first.

Chris climbed over the back and stood next to her, looking up at the massive stone carving.

"What is it?" Heather asked as she walked up.

R.O. headed straight for it.

"Ryan, stop!" Mavis said quickly. "It might not be safe."

"It's safe," came a voice from behind it.

Within a minute, a human head was sticking up over the top looking out toward them.

"Katelynn!" R.O. said.

"Hi R.O. What are you guys doing out here?" Katelynn said and finished her climb, until she was sitting on top of the stone.

"Young lady, are you safe to be sitting up there? I mean, couldn't this huge stone whatever-it-is tip over and fall?" Mavis asked as she walked closer.

"I'm perfectly safe. This is stele thirteen, I think that's the number, or maybe it's fourteen. I've been climbing on it since I was six when my grandmother brought me here for the first time," she replied.

"Don't get any ideas, Ryan," Jack said firmly.

Chris, by this time, had walked around to the back of the stele and could see the tree that had grown up behind it and the easy path to the top that Katelynn had used. She climbed down and stood in the middle of the MacGregors, saying hello again to R.O.

"Mom, this is Katelynn Komarovsko, no Komanovski," R.O. tried. "She was with Dr. North last night in the dining room."

"I remember," Mavis replied and smiled.

"It's Komarovski," Katelynn corrected. *"Priviet!* My grandmother is Tatiana Komarovski from Russia. She was the first to really understand how to translate the Mayan hieroglyphics."

"Well, greetings to you too! You don't sound Russian," Mavis said curiously.

"Like I told all of them yesterday," Katelynn said gesturing to the kids, "I moved around a lot, but spent most of my time in Houston with my grandma and grandpa Harmon."

"Then Miss Komarovski, can you tell us what this stele

has to say?" Mavis said in her professor's tone of voice.

"Yes. It's a declaration that in the year A.D. 738 the king of Quiriguá, Cuac Sky, captured and killed the king of Copán, Eighteen Rabbit," Katelynn said.

"Eighteen Rabbit. What a weird name," Heather said.

"All of the Mayans had nature names. They had their own dialect, like around here it was Mopan. But if you go just a little west it's Keckchi. And to the north it is Yucatec," Katelynn said. "The Mayan city-states in this region are Caracol, Pusilha, Nim li Punit, and Lubaantun. They may have had a strong alliance with the southern, more-powerful kings at Quiriguá and Copán to protect the canoe trade routes in the Gulf of Honduras and up by the barrier reef. The alliances between city-states were very important, because each area of what is now Central America had different natural resources to trade. It would be better for Lubaatun to have a bigger and stronger king as an ally even if they were 200 miles away.

"It seems that when Calakmul defeated Tikal and the great King Curl Nose in the Peten region of Guatemala they caused a power shift throughout the Mayan world.

"Calakmul and Tikal hated each other and fought many times and this influenced the battles between other Maya city states and changed alliances many times. Remember, the winner gets to write the history so who knows what really happened sometimes!"

"Wow, you know a lot. But what about Cancun? I like the beach there," Heather said.

"That's the Yucatec language," Katelynn answered quickly.

"You are one smart young lady," Mavis said. "Kids, take a lesson from Miss Komarovski. She didn't just get this knowledgeable overnight."

"But I did—it's genetic," Katelynn said with a sober look on her face.

Everyone raised their eyebrows in unison.

"Just kidding," Katelynn said and they all laughed.

"You had me there for a second, Katelynn," Mavis said and hugged her.

"So we must be close to the new dig," Jack said.

"Yes, we're about five kilometers from the Honduras border and one kilometer from the Motagua River. The new dig is just around the bend, about two hundred meters away," Katelynn said. "Come on R.O., let's go," she said and took off in a fast walk.

R.O. looked up at Mavis, got the O.K., and took off in a run to catch Katelynn.

Chris and Natalie started off behind them as Heather stepped back into the Toyota and sat down.

"Jack, are you driving?" Heather said and smiled.

"Yes, miss. Where shall I take you?" he replied.

"Take me to Southlake Mall for the day," Heather replied.

"You wish," Mavis said and got in.

"Yes, I do wish," Heather replied.

"Just three more stops after Belize, sweets," Mavis said.

"I know. It's not so bad. I've been hotter, wetter, dirtier, and colder than this before. I just didn't have a bump on my head," Heather replied as Jack put the Toyota in gear and drove around the bend in the road to the base of the giant Mayan temple, which was still partly covered in vines, trees, and beautiful tropical foliage.

The archaeology team was halfway-up one side with a team of locals digging through a tree trunk. They appeared to be trying to open a doorway.

"That's awesome," Heather said as she stepped out of the Toyota.

"It is impressive. Just as much as Egypt," Mavis said.

Chris, Natalie, R.O., and Katelynn were already climbing to the top of the pyramid.

"Well, let's go, Jack," Mavis said and took off.

"You coming, honey?" Jack said to Heather.

"I'm going to sit this one out today. I don't want a headache in this heat," she replied.

"Good idea. Keep watch over the goods," Jack said and walked away.

"First stop just ahead," Kim Spencer said to Mickey Banister, who had been napping.

"Good. I'm ready for a stretch," he replied.

"We're about forty miles southeast of Belmopan at Dangriga. This is the tourist trap for the ruins at Pomona and Kendal and some of the caves in the region that have petroglyphs—rock engravings. Each set of major ruins fuels the tourist economy and also the scientists that come here from all over the world to study the Maya. Each site has been staked out by a specific university, which keeps coming back every year," Spencer said.

"That would make it easy to track down who's robbing the ruins, right?" Banister asked.

"That's the catch. Not all the ruins have been affected. The only pattern I have found are the satellite kingdoms around the major Mayan centers, but only a certain number have been affected," Spencer said as she pulled up to a small cantina and got out. "Let's get something cold to drink before we go off-road."

"Works for me," Banister said.

Once inside, she continued their conversation.

"There's a theory called quadripartite cosmogony," Spencer said, as she unscrewed the cap off the bottle of water she ordered.

"That's four parts of the cosmos or something, right?" Banister said and took a swig of his drink. "Sure wish this was a brown bottle of Henry Weinhard's Gourmet Root Beer."

"Sounds delicious. Now back to the Mayans. A guy named Thomas Barthel came up with the idea that four Mayan capitals might have created a relationship of sorts. He referred to the capitals as four-directional-capitals in a quadripartite cosmogony. Cosmogony is the development of the universe, so in this case you would have four kingdoms developing at the same time and having trade or a political relationship within this 'universe,'" Spencer said.

"Yeah, but did they like each other?" Banister said and took a drink.

"No, they didn't. They fought on occasion, and in this case the quadripartite refers to Copán, Quiriguá, and Tikal," Spencer said.

"But that's just three," Banister said.

"True, and the kingdoms all speak different languages. But some scholars are saying that Calakmul qualifies as the fourth kingdom. No one knows for sure," Spencer said.

"So where's the looting pattern in relation to the quadripartite cosmogony?" Banister asked.

"The looting started high in the Maya Mountains in the west and moved to the coast. Then it started again on the barrier reef island, and is moving inland to the west," Spencer said.

She opened her big shoulder bag and pulled out a map.

"This is where we are now. Everywhere you see an 'X' is where the looters have hit," she said. "Most of them are also new discoveries."

Banister took a saltshaker and dumped a load of salt onto the map. He then took the index finger of his right hand and drew a line from Calakmul to Copán.

"Looks like three teams of looters moving east to west, with an occasional zigzag north or south. Are these dates correct?" Banister asked, noting the dates of the looting marked on the map.

"Yes, they are," Spencer replied. "Mickey, we came to the same conclusion that you're about to say. The digs last for six days straight, they move camp to another ruin, and they dig again. In four months the teams of looters have hit nearly eighty locations. We know for certain that the tombs of seven kings have been found. Mickey, that's the equivalent of a century of exploration in just 120 days."

"Kim, someone's got a map and a boatload of money to spend," Mickey said and leaned back. "You don't need a dried-up old FBI agent that Washington put out to pasture; you need a crack squad from our black ops group."

"I've been to Washington, Mexico City, Guatemala City, and London. No one wants to help. No one believes me, and the ones who do want to know what their share will be when the artifacts are recovered," Kim said.

Mickey took the last swig of his drink and set the bottle down.

"Where can I rent a chopper? I still have my FBI credit card, and I still know how to get a gun in a foreign country," Mickey said and smiled.

"There's a tourist helicopter service at Belize City on the coast at the airport," Kim said.

"Call them, give them this card number, and tell them to come get us. Tell them to book us for a week. No more hard roads for us, little lady," Mickey said, smiled, and gave his credit card to Kim.

"Special Agent Banister, you really know how to charm a lady, don't you?" Kim said.

"Just one Texan to another!" he said. "We need to get airborne if we are going to catch up with these looters. Chief Inspector Lidia and his man Proctor have their hands full with drug smuggling, so we can't expect much help from the authorities. It's spelled like Lidia but you pronounce it Lidee, right?"

"That's right. It's always confusing at first," Kim replied.

"Waiter, bring me another cold drink. We might as well eat lunch. It'll take them a couple of hours to get here. Do you serve steaks here?"

"Sí señor," the waiter said.

"Bring me the biggest one you have and burn it!" Mickey said.

8

Fierce Protector

R.O. and Katelynn tied in the race to the top of the ancient pyramid.

"Whew! I'm out of breath," R.O. admitted.

"I'm used to it. Most of the time I have cousins here with me, but this time I was lucky that Dr. North brought me along without a parent, aunt, uncle, or relative of any kind. He's an old friend of my grandmother," Katelynn said.

"I can see that you like it here," R.O. said. "It's really cool. We've been a few interesting places this year. My dad is writing a book on endangered species and he's here to talk with some scientists about the jaguar population."

"They're really beautiful. Maybe we'll spot one so you can see it. Most of the time they run away and the closest you can get is about one hundred yards from them," Katelynn said.

"Well, we saw one yesterday," R.O. said shyly.

"Tellin' her about your fight with the mother jaguar, are ya?" Natalie said as she walked up behind them.

"Is that how you got that bandage on your ear?" Katelynn said and put her hands to her mouth.

"Yep, little brother here snatched a jaguar cub and took off with it on the canopy trolley," Chris said as he walked up.

"You *what?*" Katelyn said, even more amazed. "I've never been closer than three hundred feet from one in all my life."

"Well, I'm just lucky," R.O. said, trying to act brave.

"More like you have dumb luck," Natalie threw in.

"Who's got dumb luck?" Mavis said as she reached the last step. "One could break a neck climbing these steps with all the debris still on them."

"That's why we clean them up," said Dr. North as he walked up from the other side of the temple.

"I'm David North," he said and reached out for Mavis' hand. "We met yesterday in the dining room. I assume you are Mavis MacGregor?"

"Yes, I am. Jack got diverted around to your dig on the way up," Mavis said. "Thank you for patching my son's ear yesterday."

"No problem. Our camp captain is a medical doctor this year, Dr. Craven, and she's a dandy. She can handle everything up to and including minor surgery," North said.

"That's wonderful," Mavis replied.

"Mom, I'm going to follow Katelynn around. Is that O.K.?" R.O. asked.

"Yes, honey, I assume she knows where safe is and safe isn't," Mavis said.

"Yes, she does well when it comes to safety," Dr. North said. "Her family would bury me in one of these pyramids if I let something happen to her."

"Like falling through an ancient burial chute?" Mavis asked.

"Yes, I heard about that. In my thirty years as an archaeologist, I've never seen a chute give way like that. I'm glad the kids are safe and it was a lucky find for us—a new deposit of Maya Blue," North said.

"I saw that on Ryan's boots," Mavis said.

"We've been trying to figure it out for years and finally some chemists, archaeologists, and anthropologists have come up with some ideas about it. Now we know that Mayans painted their human sacrifices blue and did so while mixing the paint ingredients in a fire beside a cenote. Your children's adventure gives us another source of the color to continue to verify its chemical ingredients," Dr. North said. "We now believe it is a combination of clay called palygorskite, indigo dye from the plant, and the special incense that the Maya burned that caused the dye and the clay to bond and keep it from fading over time."

"It's like no other blue I have ever seen," Mavis replied.

"A little turquoise in it makes it different. It's the heated, white-clay mixture that does it, I'm told," North said. "But it's also permanent, so he'll have blue boots from now on."

"He'll think that's cool," Mavis replied.

"What are you two doing?" Mavis said to Chris and Natalie.

"Just listening to the two of you," Chris said.

"And learning a lot," Natalie added.

"Well then, let's go down and see if they've got the front door to this place open yet," Dr. North said and started the descent.

As they reached the doorway, half-way down the east side, two Belizean workmen were carrying away chunks of wood from a massive tree root that had worked its way across the face of the pyramid and down the main entrance toward the center of the pyramid.

"Clear enough to proceed, Dr. North," a graduate student said and moved to the side. "The lintel is reading in the Sky Dynasty like you expected. We'll have to clean more of the glyphs, but there are signs of the Long Count."

"What's the Long Count?" Natalie asked.

"The Long Count is the continuous count of days from the Mayan creation date in August 3114 B.C.," responded Dr. North. "It's divided in units as small as 20 years, called a katun, or 400 years, known as a baktun. The Mayans counted in 20s instead of 10s. Then there are glyphs like this one here over the door," Dr. North said and pointed to the lintel.

"This one is Kankin. Then this one here is Cumku," he said as he ran his hand across the long stone lintel over the doorway. "Those are two of the months for a 365 day year, except the Mayans never could get their numbers to come out right so they had five days at the end of the year when they felt the sun god would go into darkness. They called them Hell days. Some of the modern Mayans still call them that, and have mixed this belief in with their Catholic religion."

"Amazing. Such a smart race of people," Mavis said.

"I read that the Mayans have a date when the earth will come to an end," Natalie said.

"Yes, but there is much debate over what that date is," Dr. North said.

"Yes, I've heard that too," Mavis said.

"But that's not the date we're concerned with here. This magnificent pyramid seems to be out of place. It's not aligned with the other big pyramids of the region, meaning they are not on the same star chart. The Mayans built their cities to match the star patterns they included in their religion. Everything they did was for their religion," Dr. North said. "We also have found glyphs belonging to Cuac Sky and Jade Sky, two of the last kings of Quiriguá, to the south of here. And then one of the graduate students who came down early, ahead of Camp Itzam Na, discovered a reference on a new stele found in the forest for a king named Shield Jaguar."

"Shield Jaguar, that's a cool name," Chris said.

"It literally means 'fierce protector,'" Dr. North said. "Problem is that the Jaguar kings were found further north across the mountains. That's the border with Guatemala. Bird Jaguar was an important king of that region."

"They seem to be as interesting as the Egyptian pharaohs," Natalie said.

"Probably more so because there were many kings alive at the same time in different regions, speaking different dialects, but using a common hieroglyph. That's quite a feat," Dr. North said.

"Anyone want to go in first with me?" Dr. North asked.

"Jack, you go. I'll stay here with the kids," Mavis said to her husband, who had joined the group by the door.

"I'm going too," Chris said.

"Me too," Natalie added.

"O.K., I'll go too," Mavis said coolly as she followed them inside the pyramid.

The *Calakmul Queen* pulled up anchor over the blue hole of the western Caribbean and headed for Frenchman's Cay. Ron Frost had just finished lunch when he walked into the large lounge and sat down behind a desk console that was filled with electronics. He flipped a switch and a forty-two-inch monitor arose from the back of the sofa in front of him. A map of the Mayan realm appeared on it. Mr. Frost pushed another button and a grid of red lines connected across the map, showing where each new dig site was to be found. There were blue circles around those that had been looted already. The looted sites that produced a king's tomb were highlighted in gold. First Officer Emily Hinds walked into the room.

"Mr. Frost," she said softly.

"Yes," he replied.

"A new satellite feed has just been received from our friends, the Canadians," she replied.

"And what are the results?" he said, staring at the hundreds of sites that had yet to be looted.

"All sites are looking good with the exception of the Lubaantun area. We have six sites in that region which are unknown to the world, but two have recently been penetrated by someone else," Emily said and stepped back, expecting his rage.

"Who are the intruders?" Mr. Frost said, and stood up. He felt an itch on his eyebrow and was forced to scratch it. His skin cracked and blood streamed down to his eyebrow.

"We don't know yet, sir," she said, breaking into a cold sweat.

"Then don't come back into this room until you do. Is that

clear?" he said, staring intently at the tall, slender brunette in the white officer's shirt and matching shorts.

"Yes, sir," she said and left in a hurry.

A phone on the console rang. He picked it up.

"Yes," he answered.

"Ron, I'm across the Atlantic and scheduled to land in Miami in one hour," Kiley said.

"That was fast," he replied.

"I caught a Virgin Air flight non-stop Madrid to Miami just after I left Mr. Thompson outside of Madrid," she said.

"Do you have the codex?" Mr. Frost asked.

"Yes. Didn't Bill call you?" she asked.

"He did. I was just double checking," he replied.

"I leave Miami for Cancun this afternoon and will be there by four," Kiley said.

"Good. I'll have my private jet meet you and bring you to Belize City. From there, one of my fast, high powered cigarette boats will bring you down to the *Calakmul Queen.* We're moving her to Frenchman's Cay today. A man named Seat will meet you at the hanger in Belize City," Mr. Frost said.

"I know David Seat. I thought he was your banker in Grand Cayman," Kiley said.

"He is. He's here on banking business. I'm sure he won't mind providing a greeting service for me," Mr. Frost said.

"Not for the millions you've paid him over the years," Kiley replied.

"Not over the telephone, my dear. You never know who might be listening," Mr. Frost said.

"See you soon, my love," Kiley said.

"Then we will possess all that we need to make the final move for complete domination," Frost said.

"Yes, we will," she replied and put the telephone back into the seat in front of her on the plane.

She ran her credit card back through the device, picked up the phone again, and dialed a number.

"Yes," a man's voice answered.

"I have it and will be on the *Queen* by noon tomorrow," Kiley replied.

"Good. Does he suspect anything?" the man asked.

"Not a thing," she replied and hung up the phone.

Mr. Frost picked up the console phone.

"Prepare *Bird Jaguar II* for launch in fifteen minutes," Mr. Frost said.

Chief of Staff for Frost Global Enterprises Taylor Doyle immediately got up from her console and walked out to the top deck of the *Calakmul Queen* where a Sikorsky-made Schweizer 333 helicopter was tied down. Quickly releasing the tie down straps, she opened the doors to air out the small, three-man helicopter. Hopping into the pilot's seat, she turned on the power and checked all the dials to be sure it was ready for flying. Once back down on the deck, she retrieved a bottle of glass cleaner and some white towels and began to clean the windshield across the expanse of the bubble-front aircraft. Taylor could have had any deck hand do this chore, but she took her job seriously as chief of staff and wanted to be sure it was done to Mr. Frost's standards. Once she removed all the salt deposits, she began to wipe down both sides, revealing the paint job that made the aircraft appear as if it was coated with a layer of frost with the red letters *Frost Global Enterprises.*

Ron Frost appeared from the stairs and walked over to Taylor.

"Thank you," he said and climbed aboard the Schweizer 333. He had named his helicopter after a great Mayan king, Bird Jaguar.

He was soon in the air and headed southeast at a speed of one hundred knots. At this speed, he could cruise for nearly four hours, but once over land he would reduce speed by about thirty percent to look for the landmarks revealing the ancient temples. The dependable Rolls Royce Turbine 250 engine purred like a kitten as he skimmed across the ocean one hundred feet up in the air. As he passed over the coast, he looked for the various mounds that he knew contained old temples and, inside some of them, the precious treasure of his ancestors.

Not far away, a French-made Aérospatiale helicopter set down in an open area near the cantina. A velociraptor was painted on both sides. Mickey and Kim came out of the cantina after the dust had cleared and got on board. Mickey signed the credit card receipt and the pilot tucked it away in his business satchel.

"My name is Ross Kiddie, Barrier Reef Charters. What can I do for you?" the white-haired man said.

"Mickey Banister, FBI, and this is Dr. Kim Spencer, director of antiquities for Belize," Mickey said. "We want to visit some 'off-the-charts' ruins in the area, and I've rented your chopper for one week."

"That's cool with me. I would stay busy anyhow, but this way I don't have to be a tour guide. It'll be like a vacation," Kiddie replied and chuckled.

"Are you a veteran?" Spencer asked.

"Sergeant Major, United States Army, twenty-five years," Kiddie replied.

"Excellent, then we're in good hands," Mickey replied.

"I hope so. I just got my pilot's license last summer," Kiddie replied.

"You *what?"* Kim said, aghast at the revelation.

Kiddie laughed.

"Just kidding. Been flying these whirly birds for nearly three decades. My first one was about the size of a VW bug," Kiddie replied.

"I like this size better," Kim said.

"Here's the map. We're starting at the east and will go west. We'll check for a landing spot first, and if there isn't one, then we move on to the next one," Mickey said and opened up the map.

"Can do," Kiddie replied and pushed forward on the cyclic, causing the helicopter to lift into the air. He then started humming a song as was his habit when he flew. He rotated the cyclic, causing the helicopter to spin once before moving forward.

The first stop was only forty-five minutes away by air, but four to six hours away by four-wheel drive. As the blue and gold helicopter circled a hidden temple that appeared as a hill among the tall trees, all three on board looked for a landing zone.

"I've got one," Ross said into the headpiece.

He spun the helicopter around and came in from the south. The rotary blades just barely cleared the huge trees as he set the machine down.

"How long on the ground?" Ross asked as Mickey and Kim climbed out of the aircraft.

"I don't know, maybe an hour," Kim replied.

"Suits me," Ross said and flipped all the switches to turn off the chopper.

After Mickey and Kim had left, Ross pulled out a neck pillow and his Army-issue Colt .45 pistol, which he set on the seat next to him. He then leaned back and went to sleep. He knew when to include power naps on the itinerary, but he also knew about the nasty characters that roamed the jungles of Central America so he kept his gun close.

Mickey followed Kim as she began walking the perimeter of the temple. Neither spoke as they pushed through rainforest shrubs taller than their heads and sidestepped thick vines. With Kim eight feet in front of him, Mickey took out the CZ 75, chambered a round, and clicked on the safety. Kim heard it and turned around.

"Just being on the safe side, Special Agent?" she said and smiled.

"Yes, ma'am. Be prepared is something I learned a long time before Quantico and the FBI academy," Mickey replied.

"You're my kind of man," Kim said.

"You're welcome," he replied, glad that in the shadows she couldn't see him blush.

They walked the entire north side, when they suddenly heard the flapping wings of a flock of birds. Both stopped and looked at each other. Mickey put his right index finger to his lips, signaling the need to stay quiet. Kim nodded back.

Mickey moved past her and held the gun out in front with both hands to balance for a quick shot. As they turned the corner of the temple and stepped beside a tree that had grown into the first twenty steps, they could see dirt along the temple steps and off to the side, piled as high as a small truck. There was no noise.

As Mickey moved up to the pile of dirt, a flock of parrots took off from the third tier of the rainforest canopy. Their wings made a magnificent swooshing noise like no other. As Kim looked up at the birds, Mickey flipped off the safety of the CZ 75 and looked into the deep hole that sat like a wound on the side of the magnificent temple.

"No one here now," Mickey said in a normal voice. "They must have had a small digging machine or something. This dirt is all fresh. Can't be more than a week old. None of it's packed and there aren't any leaves layered in the pile," Mickey said.

"Special Agent Banister, you make a good forensic archaeologist," Kim said.

"I've been on a few of those cases over the years," Mickey replied and leaned over to pick up something that caught his eye.

He held it in one hand and retrieved his water bottle from the sling around his neck. He poured water on it to clean away the dirt.

"Oh my," Kim said as she looked at the beauty of the gold and turquoise object jump from the dirt and clay.

"Ear piece of some kind?" Mickey asked.

"Yes, and not just anyone's earpiece. This belonged to a queen," Kim replied.

"A queen? Then there must have been a king nearby," Mickey replied.

"The queen of the jaguar god. See these marks? That's the number seven followed by the calendar day Akbal, which means night. Whoever first wore these earrings was the bride of someone who claimed to be the god of night and who dressed like a jaguar. No other woman would be allowed to wear this designation. Her king would dress in the royal skin of the jaguar, which represented the starry night of the constellation that they worshipped," Kim said.

She held the piece for Mickey to see. The ear piece was solid gold, round in shape, as was common for the Maya, and about one and a half inches across with the constellation depicted in turquoise across the face of it. The mark of 7 Akbal was at the bottom of the piece.

"You can tell all that from this piece of gold and turquoise?" Mickey said.

"Yes. And if we find more artifacts, we will know more. It breaks my heart that looters found a royal tomb and took out all that we could have studied and learned more about the Mayans," Kim replied.

"I understand," Mickey said and walked further into the gaping hole of the temple.

They both had to walk bent over through the small canal that was fashioned by the looters. Kim would reach down and pick up something every few feet and say "Oh my." Soon she was clutching two handfuls of gold, silver, jade, and turquoise.

"These guys weren't real good looters," Mickey said as he picked up a solid gold bracelet and put it on his right wrist. "Hey doc, it fits, at least until we get back to civilization."

"It's a magnificent piece, Mickey."

Suddenly, the stone wall started to vibrate.

"That's not an earthquake. It must be the looters on the other side of the temple," Kim said.

"They weren't finished. They were coming back to get it," Mickey said.

A couple of minutes passed as Kim and Mickey stood silently in the tunnel. Then they heard voices at the opening of the tunnel.

Mickey readied his CZ 75 9mm pistol.

9

Bird Jaguar II

Kiley Spencer walked across the lounge of the restaurant with the Codex of Madrid still secure in its waterproof case, tucked inside the black, leather carry-on bag that she rolled behind her. Scanning the restaurant, she finally spied the person she was looking for behind a newspaper at a table overlooking the marina. Exhausted from the flight from Madrid to Miami to Cancun to Belize City, she wore crumpled, cotton pants and a loose-fitting, blue, cotton blouse. Flip flops and a straw hat on her red hair made her look like a tourist. As she approached, the man lowered the paper and looked up.

"Glad you made it," Seat said casually without getting up. He looked at her over the top of his $600 designer sunglasses.

"Me too," Kiley replied and sat down, pulling the case closer to her until it touched her right leg.

"How were your flights?" Seat asked.

"Now David, do you really care or are you just being polite?" she replied.

"You're right, I don't care. I could care less if you were

bumped around like a popcorn kernel in a kettle or if you got so sick you threw up your guts for hours. All I want to know is if the object in that case is the Codex," he said and put the paper down.

"Now, that's more like the cutthroat I've grown to love and hate at the same time," Kiley replied.

"Thank you, my dear. But if it's love you want, Sir Philip is your man and I can see you are still angry about our little job in Barbados," Seat replied snidely.

"If my cut on this job wasn't in the millions, you would be shark food by now," Kiley said.

"Ah, your youth speaks out," Seat said and looked her straight in the eye. "When you're angry, you are just that much more beautiful. Does Sir Philip tell you that?" Seat asked, antagonizing her.

"Philip is lucky to be alive, no thanks to you. You were supposed to pay off two of Frost's men so he could escape. If my girl Taylor hadn't been there to orchestrate it, he would be in the bottom of the sea," Kiley said as a waiter walked up. She ordered coffee, black.

"If you remember, Taylor used to work for me. She's very reliable so let's put that behind us. Frost has the key to the lost treasure of the Mayan kings and we can't let petty personal grievances get between us and the biggest treasure find since King Tut, now can we?" Seat said, and calmly drank some orange juice as if this were just another money transfer to his Cayman Island bank for a client hiding money from the IRS. He put the glass down as Kiley's coffee was delivered. The waiter walked away.

"Now where is Frost and his yacht?" Seat asked.

"You mean *my* yacht," Kiley said, taking a sip of her coffee and savoring the strong Caribbean brew.

"Exactly. Yours, theirs, I really don't care. I just want the Codex that Frost showed Sir Philip—the one from France—the Jesuit Codex. That's the map to the riches he has been looting across the Mayan world. Get it and I'll give you my biggest castle in Scotland and a new Cessna Citation jet to go with it," he said, staring at her with his steel gray eyes.

"That's not going to be easy. I assume he has it under lock and key," Kiley said.

"Sir Philip told me the key is around his wrist," Seat replied.

"That makes it even more difficult. But there is no way that he was able to track down those lost temples without digitizing all the documents. He had to have scanned them, and then downloaded a program that matched the sites with the available satellite maps of the area," Kiley said. "Someone is doing his satellite work and we need to find them, too. I've heard him mention that someone in Canada is helping him."

"Treasure tracking is your gig, my dear. I'm just here to fence the stuff after you take it from Frost and kill him. If that's what you modern archaeologists do, then I suggest you get into his main computer and simply e-mail me the map," Seat said.

"He guards that like his safe," she responded. "But first a cup of coffee, a Dramamine, and then let's find Ron's boat."

"It's the yellow one near the end of the dock," Seat said.

"Beautiful cigarette boat," she replied, looking out the large window.

"Yes it is. I prefer the more graceful boats so one can enjoy the ride. Those cigarette boats are nothing more than maritime's version of fast food. A thoroughly cooked Beef Wellington is much more enjoyable," Seat said.

"I will have to forego more company and just take the Dramamine. Wouldn't want to raise any suspicion that we know each other, would we?" Kiley said, leaned over, and kissed him on the forehead. "If you hadn't beat me out of half a million, I might like you better than Sir Philip. Give my regards to the wife."

"Oh, I will my dear. She and the children are on holiday in the Greek Isles," he said.

"Tell her to enjoy it, because soon her allowance will be cut in half after you buy me that castle," Kiley said with fire in her eyes.

"Bon voyage," Seat said and winked back.

"Yes, sir. I see a redhead coming down the pier right now, sir. Yes, she has in her hand a carry-on bag. Wheels don't work so well on the wood, sir. Yes, sir. I will, sir," the cigarette boat pilot said into the cell phone. He put it into his chest pocket and pulled the Velcro flap down tight.

"Dr. Spencer?" he said as she walked up to the boat.

"I am," Kiley replied.

"This is Mr. Frost's boat. Can I get your bag?" he said.

"Yes. Please put it below and tie it down. It can't be jostled around," Kiley responded and climbed up the short ladder into the boat after handing over the bag.

Once on board, she walked aft into the small kitchen and found a refrigerator. Taking out a bottle of something very strong, she took a big swig and walked back to the outer deck as the pilot fired up the big engines.

"Frenchman's Cay in three hours," he said.

"I thought these boats go eighty miles per hour," Kiley said and frowned.

"Yes doctor, they do. But we're traveling inside the barrier reef, and if we closed in on a reef at that speed I wouldn't have time to make the correction. We'd either become airborne or cut in half," he replied and smiled.

"Slower is better," Kiley said. "Besides, I could use the sun time," she said and took off her blouse, revealing the top half of her floral-print bikini. Soon she was rubbing coconut oil on her skin and thinking about the riches that would be hers some day. She wouldn't need Patterson or Seat and she could call her own shots, and yes, Bill Thompson's skill would come in handy. She knew that Kim would understand, somehow—she hoped.

Mickey and Kim leaned up against the ancient stone of the pyramid and stood as still as a spider trying to avoid the eyes of a predator. The voices got louder and louder until they could see silhouettes of two men walking, the lighted entrance behind them.

"I think they went in here," said one man.

Mickey stepped out, thinking that the voice belonged to their pilot, Ross Kiddie.

"Sergeant Major, is that you?" Mickey said.

"There you are," Kiddie replied.

"We thought you might be the looters returning. Then we heard a noise and felt a vibration through the stone," Kim said.

"It was this fine gentleman," Kiddie said. "This is Mark Taylor. He's the land owner around this temple."

"Con mucho gusto," Mickey said and put his gun away, offering to shake the man's hand.

"Mr. Taylor is from Belfast. He told me he was clearing the trees around the temple when the looters came through the forest in two large trucks. One of the trucks had a tractor with digging equipment on the front end," Kiddie said and turned to the man again.

After a couple of minutes of conversation, he turned back to Mickey and Kim.

"They worked for ten hours and then suddenly left. I was hiding in the forest nearby and watched the whole thing. They drove to this part of the temple and then just started burrowing into the side as if they knew exactly which stone to take out first," Taylor said in his strong Irish accent.

"Butchers. Nothing but historical butchers!" Kim said strongly.

"Say, you guys hit the jack pot!" Kiddie said, just noticing the gold in Kim's hands.

"Yes, this was just lying on the tunnel floor where they dug. But we better get out of here. Those braces don't look too strong," Mickey said.

"What was the vibration we heard?" Kim asked.

"It was Mr. Taylor's tractor on the east side of the pyramid. He was pulling trees away from the temple. He heard us land and came to investigate. He knows this site is little known and wants to promote it for tourism," Kiddie said.

"Smart man. Now let's get out of the tunnel," Mickey said and started walking toward the entrance.

"Mr. Taylor, would you like to accompany us to the helicopter so we can inventory these artifacts?" Kim asked.

"Yes, that would be dandy," Taylor replied.

Twenty minutes later they were back in the air in search of another lost pyramid of the Mayans.

Seventy-five miles away, archaeologist David North led the MacGregors through a series of small passageways, some coming to a dead end, dropping ten to twenty feet, or requiring them to climb up flat-faced walls with only tiny hand-holds to grasp.

"Jack MacGregor, I swear that since I agreed to come along on this trip I have spent half my life in a hole or tunnel of some kind," Mavis said in a whispering voice to Jack a few feet away.

"Sorry honey, but this is what we do," Jack replied.

"I've dug up more than one hundred dinosaurs and never went in a cave or tunnel," Mavis said back.

"Are your parents arguing?" Natalie said to Chris.

"Yup. Something that all parents do," Chris replied.

Mavis heard the comments and decided that she had said enough.

Dr. North climbed over the top of a ledge and stopped. The others approached and joined him, and soon they were all resting and drinking water.

"Looks like a dead end," Dr. North said.

"Are these temples always such a maze?" Natalie asked.

"Sometimes. We're lucky if we even have a tunnel of any kind. Most of the time, we have to move tons of stone to make a tunnel. Generally they had passageways that led to living quarters and then the tombs were sealed deep below the pyramid. I thought that because the opening we found was halfway up one side, it could lead to a royal tomb. But this time it appears that the wall we climbed was actually the wall of the first building on this site, and then the pyramid was built around that first structure. The Mayans did that a lot. One king would build something then another would build on top of it," North said.

"I'm for getting some sunlight," Natalie said and then whispered to herself. "Why did I want to come back inside one of these?"

"What's that?" Chris asked from a few feet away.

"Lead the way out," she replied.

Soon all of them were standing out in the bright sunlight, shaking off the feeling of claustrophobia and breathing fresh air.

"Jack, I'm off to find the little ones," Mavis said and started climbing back to the top of the temple.

"O.K., love," Jack replied and brushed some dirt off his khaki shorts.

Chris looked up as he heard the palpitating noise of a helicopter. Soon everyone was watching as a blue and gold Aérospatiale circled the temple mound.

"Look, over there," Chris replied. "Another chopper."

"That's a tiny one and it's flying much lower," Natalie replied.

Ron Frost could see the Aérospatiale dead ahead and took a wide circle to watch it come down in a clear spot next to the temple.

"What are you doing in my kingdom?" he said and pointed the *Bird Jaguar II* toward the landing zone.

Before the people on the Aérospatiale could disembark, Frost set the Schweizer 333 down right next to them and cut the power to the engine.

"We've got a lot of company all of a sudden," Dr. North said as he stepped from the bowels of the pyramid.

Two of his graduate students came from the side and stood next to him.

"Well Sergeant Major, we're getting out for a bit," Mickey said inside the Aérospatiale.

"Gotcha' sir. It's time for another power nap, so I'll be waiting right here," Kiddie replied. He then tuned up with his "mouth horn" and leaned back.

By the time Mickey and Kim had touched the ground, Mr. Frost was already out of his small helicopter and walking toward them. Mickey reached under his shirt and took the CZ 75 off safety.

"May I introduce myself," Mr. Frost said with a smile on his face. "I am Ron Frost, president of Frost Global Enterprises."

"And I am Dr. Kim Spencer, temporary chief of archaeology and antiquities for Belize," Kim replied and shook his hand.

"I'm Special Agent Mickey Banister, FBI," Mickey said and offered his hand.

Mr. Frost was slow to reach for it but finally did and spoke.

"Pleased to meet you Special Agent. A long way from home, aren't you?" Mr. Frost said.

"Where there is crime that affects American citizens, the FBI will be there, sir," Mickey said.

"Well put," Mr. Frost replied.

As he was finishing his sentence, Jack and Dr. North walked up.

"I am Dr. David North and this is a licensed archaeological site, which means that it is limited to air traffic by permission only. I don't remember giving permission to anyone," Dr. North said firmly.

"I'm sorry Dr. North. I'm Dr. Kim Spencer with the . . ."

"Oh yes. I remember the name. You signed our Camp Itzam Na permit," Dr. North said.

"Yes, and I am sorry we didn't tell you we were dropping in, but we didn't know until about an hour ago when we chartered this helicopter," Kim replied, her red hair shining in the sun.

"But that doesn't explain the little chopper and this gentleman," Dr. North said.

"Let me introduce myself, please. I am Ron Frost of Frost Global Enterprises, and I was just flying around and decided to follow this big helicopter into the landing zone. I assumed it was an approved landing site," Mr. Frost said, lying easily.

"I'm sorry Mr. Frost, but it is a restricted area," Dr. North said.

"Wait, are you the Ron Frost who is a millionaire collector of Mayan artifacts?" Kim asked, stepping closer and squinting her eyes.

"I am," Mr. Frost replied.

"Dr. North, there are many stories about how this man has illegally acquired Mayan artifacts on the black market," Kim said.

"Madam, I assure you all of the artifacts in my collection are legal," Mr. Frost said defensively.

Chris, Natalie, Mavis, R.O., and Katelynn walked up to the group and stood listening. R.O. was moving about trying to get a look at everyone when he suddenly stopped. He turned quickly to Mavis.

"I know that guy," he said pointing to Mickey.

"How in the world could that be?" Mavis whispered in disbelief.

"No, Mom, listen. I know that guy," he said louder.

Hearing the conversation behind him, Jack left the front of the group and walked back to his family.

"You guys keep it down," he said to them all.

Chris and Natalie moved around to the other side of the group.

"Dad, I know that guy," R.O. said again.

R.O. left his parents, walked around to the other side, and stood behind Mickey.

"Deadshot 44," R.O. said loudly.

Mickey turned around and looked down into R.O.'s face.

"Well, look what the cat drug out of the rainforest," Mickey said.

"He doesn't know how truthful that is," Natalie said and laughed.

"Ryan O'Keefe MacGregor, how goes it little fella'?" Mickey said and reached out to shake hands with R.O.

R.O. instead leaned forward and gave him a big hug. Mickey wrapped his big arms around R.O. and lifted him off the ground. The whole crowd was watching; R.O.'s family stared in amazement at the reunion. Mickey set R.O. on the ground and turned to everyone.

"This here little guy and me, well we brought down a terrorist right out of the sky," he said.

"We sure did," R.O. said with a smile from ear to ear.

"What brings your family to this hot country? It's a long way from Alaska," Mickey said.

"Just looking at more wildlife for Dad's book," R.O. said

"Still have that rifle I gave you?" Mickey said.

"Sure do. Shipped it back to Texas to go hunting with next fall in South Texas near Alpine," R.O. said.

Mr. Frost was quietly soaking in all of the information about the MacGregor family, the FBI Special Agent, the head of Belizean antiquities department, and the site, while the reunion unfolded. According to his records, this site had a king's tomb deep inside with riches untold. He also surmised that no one had found it yet. But that day would come soon, and if anyone present got in his way, he would leave them where the king had been laying for the past one thousand years.

Suddenly, R.O. and Katelynn came up behind him. He sensed someone's presence and turned around quickly, startling the two kids.

"And who do we have here?" he said as if they were six or seven years old.

"We're both teenagers so there's no need to treat us like babies," R.O. said curtly.

"I see. My apologies please," Mr. Frost answered.

"No problem. Cool little helicopter," Katelynn said looking at the 333.

"Yes, she is and fun to fly," Mr. Frost said.

"It's a she?" R.O. asked.

"Yes, it seems more appropriate when asking it to fly faster or stay in the air longer," Mr. Frost said.

"I agree with that logic," Katelynn said.

"And just what is your family doing here?" Mr. Frost asked R.O.

At that moment, blood started to drip down the side of his neck, and R.O. and Katelynn stepped back two feet. Mr. Frost could feel the warm stream but chose to ignore it. R.O. stammered as he summed up who they were and what they were doing in Central America on the eighth stop of their world journey, embellishing his role for Katelynn's benefit.

"That's impressive. You didn't say where you were staying," Mr. Frost said as he took out a handkerchief and wiped the blood away, causing a lesion on his hand to open and leak fluid across his knuckles.

"We're at the birders' resort right now but we might be moving to a place in the Maya Mountains tomorrow. Seems there are more jaguars there," R.O. said.

"He got wounded by a jaguar claw yesterday," Katelynn added. "Nearly tore his ear off."

"And it didn't hurt a bit," R.O. added.

"I'll vouch for everything he says," Mickey said as he walked up.

"I see," Mr. Frost said, sizing up the middle-aged FBI agent.

"Haven't heard of Frost Enterprises before," Mickey said.

"We are a quiet and very private company," Mr. Frost said.

"And that's why you drop in on remote Mayan temples in your own little helicopter?" Mickey asked, not liking what he was feeling about Mr. Frost.

"I have a small interest in collectables and because I was in the area and I saw the other helicopter, I presumed you to be tourists, and I thought I would just drop in for a 'look see,'" Mr. Frost said. "As a matter of fact, it's getting late in the afternoon and I should go."

"Nice meeting you, Frost. I have a feeling we'll meet again, soon," Mickey said in a firm tone.

"We'll see, Special Agent. We'll see," Mr. Frost said and turned to walk toward his helicopter.

The group watched the quiet little silver helicopter lift off and quickly fly over the top of the rainforest and disappear.

"I don't like that man," Kim said out loud.

"My vibration meter was off the scale," Mickey followed.

"Well, I've got to get my students out of the temple and on the way to Camp Itzam Na before dark. Tomorrow we're looking at a ruin where an intact ball court has been found. Chris, are you interested in a new Mayan game?" Dr. North asked.

"You bet," Chris replied.

"This I've got to see," Natalie said and smiled.

10

"Seven"

By nightfall, Sergeant Major Ross Kiddie (ret.) had flown Special Agent Banister and Dr. Spencer back to Belmopan in his chopper, named *Raptor,* and each had found a comfortable room for the night. The MacGregors and Natalie Crosswhite had returned to the birder resort and were exhausted from their long day on the Mayan roads.

Dr. Kiley Spencer had arrived at Frenchman's Cay aboard the fast cigarette boat in time to see the *Bird Jaguar II,* piloted by Ron Frost, land on the top deck of the *Calakmul Queen.*

As Mr. Frost walked across the top deck, Kiley was standing there in a soft cotton dress suitable for the tropics, her red hair glowing in the evening sun.

"Well, you finally decided to come home," she said to Mr. Frost.

"And the codex?" Mr. Frost asked.

"No hellos or whatever?" Kiley responded.

"The codex," Mr. Frost repeated.

"It's downstairs in your office in the case," Kiley said with a look of irritation on her face.

Mr. Frost walked past her and went down two flights of

stairs to the big lounge, which housed his office on one side in a smaller room. Once there he opened the black vinyl case and pulled out another case that was made for museum documents.

He reached into one of his desk drawers and found a package that contained a sterile pair of cotton gloves. He ripped open the package,pulled the gloves on, and opened the museum case surrounding the codex.

"At last, I have them all," Frost said.

"What about the Dresden Codex?" Kiley asked, walking into the room and sitting in a soft plush chair.

"Mr. Thompson called earlier this afternoon and said the Dresden Codex was in his possession," Mr. Frost said.

"Wow, Bill got there fast and pulled off the job?" Kiley said.

"He didn't say who pulled off the job, just that he had it," Mr. Frost said, never looking away from the Codex of Madrid. "The Madrid Codex is here before us. The Paris Codex is in my vault downstairs, and Dresden is on the way, as we speak," Frost said. "We can do without the artifacts from London, for now."

"Then what's left to do? I mean, you have all of the written material of the Mayans in existence. Can't you just go and get all the remaining treasure now?" Kiley asked.

"There is one thing I have not shared with you, my dear," Mr. Frost said to the red-haired beauty.

"What is it?" she replied.

"The Jesuit Codex, the one with the locations of all the tombs across the Mayan lowlands, has references to locations that are found in the other three codices. Modern names that archaeologists have assigned to the various temple mounts sometimes don't match the Mayan names in the codices. And then there are the ones that archaeologists know nothing about. From what I have learned from the Jesuit Codex, I believe one of the kings of six kingdoms of Peten state and Belize was a warlord who challenged all the other states. His aggressiveness allowed him to accumulate an amazing amount of wealth, mostly in gold and jade," Mr. Frost said.

"Why didn't you share that with me?" Kiley said.

"Some things are better kept close to the vest. It's common knowledge that the rulers of Tikal, Uaxactun, Calakmul, and Aquateca were invaded by neighboring kingdoms at varying times in their existence, but what about the forest kingdoms of the Maya Mountains or the Rio Bravo? I could spend ten years sending my looters from one archaeological site to another and still never find the largest accumulation of Mayan wealth. By this time tomorrow, this codex will be scanned into my computer. Mr. Thompson will have his done by then as well and will e-mail me the results," Mr. Frost said.

"Then why did I have to go to Madrid and risk my life and freedom stealing that codex when Bill could have done it without me?" Kiley said, getting up out of the chair, obviously becoming agitated.

"Loyalty," Mr. Frost said. "I needed to be sure I could trust you."

She moved closer to him, pushed his arms open, and kissed him.

"You know you can trust me," she said softly.

"I know that now," Frost said and turned back toward the codex. "Besides, you needed to invest something into the project. You invested risking of your life and now the reward will be that much sweeter. What's that silly cliché people say, 'no pain, no gain'? It's really true and you should know it. Besides, wasn't it a thrill floating up and over the buildings of downtown Madrid, knowing that at any second the balloon could fail and you would fall and impale yourself on the sharp points of the wrought iron fence?" Mr. Frost said.

"You knew all along?" Kiley asked.

"No, Bill told me on the phone this afternoon in the helicopter," Mr. Frost replied.

He looked across the mountains of southern Belize as the sun began to drop.

"It's almost time for the Akbal 1 ceremony," Mr. Frost said and walked out of the room.

Kiley walked to the large window that looked across the aft deck and felt the urge to call Sir Philip, but she knew it was too risky. He needed to know about the last codex. Tomorrow might find a better moment.

Thirty minutes later the sky was nearly black and Mr. Frost emerged from the lounge onto the aft deck of the massive yacht wearing only black swim trunks. Two assistants prepared an area for the ceremony by placing three hundred burning candles all around the gunnels and in a circle on the teak deck.

Mr. Frost bent over, opened a wooden chest, and pulled out a rolled skin of three jaguars that had been sewn together and cut to be a mantle. He draped the mantle over his shoulders and picked up an ancient Mayan flute. An assistant handed him a Mayan king's headdress made of prized quetzal feathers. He put on the headdress and stepped inside the circle. He looked to the heavens, spied the constellation of the Bear, turned to an aide, and nodded. She took a brush out of an exquisite Mayan vase found at Seibal and flicked blood from inside it across his face. She did this three times and then stepped back into the shadows.

Mr. Frost, now covered with drops of blood, wrapped in the skin of the jaguar gods, and bearing the kingly crown of quetzal feathers, began to play the flute and sway back and forth.

Kiley watched from the darkness of the lounge. The three hundred candles created an eerie light, and their smoke began to settle on the deck so that she could not see Mr. Frost's legs from the knee down.

He began to speak.

"The offering I have brought to thee is in truth not much and will not satisfy you, oh jaguar god. On this day of Akbal 1, I come to see you off in your journey through the night and promise that when you come back to us, I will have devised a plan to bring you the sacrifices that you need to satisfy your thirst for blood and human flesh so that we can live under your protection. This very day your children sleep not far from me, and within seven days I will bring them to you. Oh jaguar god, I am committing myself to you and the number you protect—seven. Within seven days, you will taste the blood of your children and will rejoice with Kukulcan and Xipe Totec who are hungry for the flayed skin of a human," Mr. Frost shouted to the stars in the darkness above. His two female aides appeared from the darkness, dancing around the ring of fire.

As Mr. Frost continued to speak, he reached out into the darkness beyond the candles and an aide appeared out of the darkness with an eight-foot-long albino python coiled around her body. She stepped inside the ring of smoke and light and the snake began to reach out toward Mr. Frost until its head was touching his shoulder. Within seconds, the giant snake moved to wrap itself around Mr. Frost and attempt to squeeze him to death. It slithered under his arms, around his neck, and down to his legs. Mr. Frost continued playing the flute for a moment and then spoke.

"May Ix Chel, the goddess of the moon whom you adore, guide you through the dominion of the nine lords of the night, the Bolon-ti-Ku, and may the sun greet you with prosperity for seven more days. Because, oh lord, I promise that within seven days I will bring to you what you have thirsted for since my mother Zak Kuk ruled Calakmul twelve centuries ago. It is her blood that fills my body and leads me to you. It is her strength that carries me through the day with the invaders who destroyed your temples, killed your people, and burned the sacred maize. Oh, my lord, my heart aches from the loss of the maize, which fed us and protected us until the invaders came and destroyed our way of life. Zak Kuk will rise again through me and reign over the kings of the forests, and I will bring pain to the Europeans, at last," Mr. Frost shouted again into the night.

"Oh powerful lord of the night, I will bring to you the

ones whose names I will write into the wood of the forest," Mr. Frost said and took a rare obsidian knife, which he had recovered from a king's tomb, from a scabbard on the inside of the jaguar skin.

He reached down to his waist to where the powerful white snake had positioned its head, ready to squeeze the life out of him. With one quick motion, he severed the head of the snake. Holding the head in his left hand, he leaned over to the teak-wood deck and wrote out two names. He then pulled the dead snake from his body and slung it over the gunwale into the ocean. Kiley gasped, but she could not be heard from within the protection of the lounge. Mr. Frost then lay down on the bloody deck and closed his eyes, swimming in the blood of the snake. An aide walked over to him and pulled the jaguar skin completely over his body. Then she began distinguishing the flames on all of the candles. The blotted names of the sacrifices could barely be seen as Mr. Frost rolled to one side: *Ryan and Katelynn.*

When the morning light came, Ron Frost awoke from his trance, still lying on the deck wrapped in the jaguar skin. He was now one day closer to pleasing the god of the forest and the night, the lord jaguar, with the blood of R.O. and Katelynn. Noticing that his skin was cracking from his disease and his blood emerging, Mr. Frost quickly headed for the cooling chamber where he would spend two hours.

That same morning, safe in the birder camp, R.O. got up and followed Chris to the dining hall for a "healthy breakfast," as Mavis had declared to all. High up in Camp Itzam Na, Katelynn Komarovski joined several scientists for bacon and eggs as a cool breeze blew through the camp. Neither R.O. nor Katelynn knew what the next seven days would bring or that they were marked to please Xipe Totec in his thirst for human blood. All they had in mind was just another day exploring new temples and the beautiful rain forest.

Mr. Frost sat quietly in the cooling chamber as the classical music played loudly. Dried blood had caked all over his back. His mind was focused on how he would fulfill his destiny as the new King of the Mayans and how he would use his vast empire to destroy Spain and all the European nations who had invaded the homeland of his mother, Zak Kuk. He opened his eyes suddenly. He couldn't decide who should die first!

11

The Ball Court

The MacGregors were back on the road again and driving toward the Mayan ruin complex north of Xnaheb, a twenty-minute drive from the birder camp and Camp Itzam Na, high in the hills of the Maya Mountains on the Grande River. Up too early, the kids were resting the best they could in the open-air Toyota and in the early morning humidity. R.O. was munching on a chocolate pastry that resembled an American donut, much to his mother's chagrin. Mavis had grown tired of arguing about healthy breakfasts every day on the road. So she felt it was time to give in to a childish desire and ate one with him.

"Good donut, Mom," R.O. said from the seat behind her.

"I agree; it's pretty good. I can taste the giant fat molecules in every bite and feel them rush down to my thighs," Mavis replied.

"Oh, Mom, please!" Heather replied. "You are in such good shape. I mean look at all the athletic things you do."

"Yea, Mom, you look great!" Chris threw in.

"I just hope I can look as good as you do when I'm fifty," Natalie said.

"Fifty! I beg your pardon," Mavis said indignantly.

Jack and the kids started laughing.

"Just kidding, just kidding," Natalie replied still laughing.

"Pyramid site number eighteen dead ahead, and it looks like we're all alone at the moment," Jack said from the driver's seat.

"Just why are we here today?" Mavis asked.

"The Guatemalan and Belizean wildlife specialists are coming to meet here for two days to discuss the jaguar population in the park. It appears that landowners are beginning to encroach into jaguar habitat at an alarming rate. It's a good time for me to meet folks from both sides of the border," Jack replied. "And Dr. North and his people are going to be here to study the ball court. He has some grad students who have never seen one."

"Good thinking, Dad," Heather said as she reached for another pastry.

The Toyota came to a stop and Mavis got out and rounded up all the teens next to the vehicle.

"Well, I have some good news and some bad news," Mavis said.

"Mom, can't this wait until we get back to the lodge tonight?" R.O. said.

"No, it's going to happen now, so listen," she replied. "I've given you a reprieve from your school work for over a month now, and it's time to get back to it. If you're lucky, maybe Natalie will help you with it."

"Not me. I graduated high school already," Natalie replied, and then noticed the stare that Mavis was sending her way. "Well, maybe I can help out a little bit."

"Your assignment this week is to find the ball court at these ruins and go through a simulated game of Pok-Ta-Pok. I brought a couple of books, which are in the food basket, that will help you figure it out. Then over the next few days, I want you to write a three-page paper about the game and why it had importance to the Mayan religion," Mavis said. "Does anyone have any questions? Oh, I forgot, the ring for you to throw the ball through is twenty feet off the ground with only a nineteen inch opening."

"A ball game . . . can't be that bad. Where's the ball?" R.O. said.

"That's for you to figure out, young man," Mavis said. "The ruins are that way. Stay together at all times. Got it, Ryan?"

He walked a few steps away and turned.

"Yes, Mom. I got it. I will be the perfect child today," R.O. replied and turned to catch up with the others. They picked up the two books, grabbed their packs, and headed down the trail toward the ruins.

"And perfect you will be, little brother," Chris said when he reached them, "Or I will tell Katelynn about all the dumb stuff you do all the time."

"Hey!" R.O. said and gave Chris a dirty look.

"A new weapon. I like that," Natalie added.

Parked a hundred yards away was a small, subcompact car with rust marks all over its faded, blue exterior. Two men were sitting in it. One put a telephone to his mouth.

"Boss?" he said.

Ron Frost stood on the top deck of the *Calakmul Queen* and answered the phone.

"Yes, go ahead," Mr. Frost replied.

"We followed them to the new site northwest of Xnaheb. Looks like a day trip or something. The adults are going a different direction from the kids. The boy is here but the girl isn't. She's still up in the tree camp, as far as we can tell."

"Let me know when she's on the move. We have six days left to get them in the same spot. I'll be there as soon as I can," Mr. Frost said and hung up.

He climbed aboard the compact Schweizer 333 helicopter and within minutes was cruising across the aquamarine waters off the coast of Belize toward the new archaeological site twenty miles northwest of Frenchman's Cay.

"Here's a picture of a ball court," Natalie said, holding the book out for all to see.

The group stopped in the shade of a tree, passed the book around, and then began walking again. Natalie kept reading from the book.

"You guys, it says that there was a king named Cauac Sky and he had a battle with King Eighteen Rabbit from another Mayan city named Copán, which it says is about 150 miles south of here and much bigger. So the Sky dude captures the Rabbit dude and lops his head off to become the new super-king of the region," Natalie said.

"So just the kings fought, and whoever won wins the war?" R.O. asked.

"No, that would be too simple and logical. Do you think they would do that today? So there was a nasty war and the Cauac Sky king captures the Copán king. Seems it was part of a political alliance between two other cities to the north named Tikal and Calakmul," Natalie replied. "It says that Sky king had a lot of riches from the jade trade and the river we drove by. But, wait, there was a flood and that changed everything."

"There's the opening to the ruins area," Heather said as they continued to walk while Natalie read.

"What are those tall rocks?" R.O. asked.

"That must be it over there," Chris said.

The kids walked around for nearly two hours before they stopped on a hill looking down on a large and beautiful courtyard covered with grass. Archaeologists, graduate students, and helpers had cleared the dirt, debris, tree roots, and rocks from a small area of the ball court where the stone circle was attached to the wall. Grass covered the rest of the court and the observers' seats on each side.

"Mom must have been faking it again," R.O. said. "I don't see a ball court."

"No, she wasn't faking it. There was a ball court here once and people played the ball game on it," Chris replied as he found a spot to sit on the ancient steps.

"Seems that the purpose of the game they called Pok-Ta-Pok was to place a rubber ball through a stone ring mounted twenty-feet up on the side of a wall of the court. The teams had uniforms that were colorful and protective. Sounds to me like field hockey without a stick," Chris said.

"That's too simplistic, Chris," Natalie interrupted and looked down at her book. "Let me tell you how it was played. First the game originated when the Xibalba, the bad guys of the underworld, got tired of the noise from the ball court of the people on the earth above them and challenged them to a game in the underworld. But it was a trick and they cut off the heads of the two brothers who went to the underworld to play them. Oh, the two brothers were also the children of the first creators of the earth."

"This is deep," R.O. said and leaned back in the sun.

"Well, well. Apparently one of the killed brothers becomes the father of a child born to a Xibalban woman by spitting in her hand . . ."

"What? Are you kidding?" Chris said.

"No. According to legend, his head was hanging in a tree in the underworld and he spit into her hand as she walked by. You have to realize that these are all myths. Greek mythology can sound just as weird too, sometimes," Natalie said. "Let me go on.

"Well the underworld woman had twins and these two people are called the Hero Twins because they fooled the Xilbalbans, the bad dudes, into sacrificing themselves," she said.

"How dumb were they?" R.O. said.

"Shut up," Chris said softly, not wanting a return remark.

"So the Hero Twins, representing the living world, gained power over the underworld," Natalie said. "Now here are the rules. First you can wear equipment, and I'll skip over that part, but it says there are pictures of players and equipment around each ball court."

R.O. rolled to his left and stared at the stone carving.

"Here's a guy with a helmet and some gear around his waist and his shoes. He looks different that the other ones we've seen," he said. "Looks pretty cool to me. I bet the ball players were like the pro football and soccer players of the day. They got the best houses, best food—you know—real celebrities."

"R.O., you are weirding out on us," Chris said and smiled.

"Back to the game . . . the ball is solid rubber, may weigh as much as ten pounds, and bounces easily. Let's see, the goal is to get the ball through the other team's hoop, or stone circle, as they call it. Wow, you won't believe this," Natalie said.

"What?" Heather said from her prone position as she lay tanning on a step.

"You could use your arms, legs, hips, belly, back, and head, but you couldn't use your hands," Natalie said.

"That's a tough shot from twenty feet down," Chris said.

"But the book says you can also score by getting the ball into the end zone . . ."

"Like football!" R.O. said loudly. "I knew it. My team will be the Calakmul Cowboys!"

"No, not like football, because if you didn't touch the ball after the second bounce, then it would count as a score," Natalie said. "But there's a catch. If the game were played because a god was sad, mad, or in need of a sacrifice, then the winning team's captain got his head chopped off."

"No way. You're making that up," R.O. said and sat up quickly.

"Nope. Read it right here if you don't believe me," Natalie replied.

"So let me get this right. Get it through the ring, don't touch it by the second bounce, or get it to the opposing team's end zone and you win, or rather, you lose," Chris said.

"That's it," Natalie answered.

"I nominate R.O. for our team captain," Heather said and smiled.

"I second that nomination," came a voice from the top of the stairs.

"Katelynn! Good to see you, girl. When did you get here?" Natalie said and stood up.

"Just a few minutes ago. Dr. North told me where to find the ball court, so I came right over," Katelynn said.

"We walked around for two hours! Mom did it to us again," Heather mumbled.

Katelynn opened her backpack and tossed the rubber ball to Chris, who caught it easily.

"That's heavy," he replied.

"Bounce it," she said.

Chris stood up, walked over to the cleared area of the stone ball court, and dropped the solid rubber ball. It bounced back to waist-level easily. On the second try, he tossed it down harder and it soared over his head.

"That's amazing," he said.

"No air bladder in the ball, because air hadn't been discovered yet," Katelynn said.

"They didn't know about air?" R.O. said incredulously.

"No. That didn't come until the eighteenth century when scientists figured out what air and oxygen are," Katelynn replied. "One was British and the other was Swedish."

"It bounces great, but I would hate to get hit in the face, so I guess heading the ball is out," Chris said.

"Hey guys," one of Dr. North's graduate students said as they topped the hill and came down to the court.

"Let's divide up and try to play," Katelynn said.

"I'll keep score," Heather said, sitting up and noticing the handsome male graduate students' bronzed bodies as they took off their shirts for the game.

Soon Katelynn, Natalie, Chris, R.O., and the two male graduate students were frivolously kicking, knocking, and bumping the ball around, but with no one even coming close to the ring. They all wildly bumped the ball until it would roll freely down the grass court to the end zone and one team declared themselves the winner.

"Yes, boss. They're all in a game of Pok-Ta-Pok. Yes, both of the younger kids are here. Good. We'll keep an eye on them until you get here," the man said from his vantage point beyond the ball court.

Mr. Frost circled high so as to avoid attention and landed the relatively quiet, small helicopter about two hundred yards from the ball court and a good half-mile from the other scientists and Mavis MacGregor. Jack MacGregor had already left for the jaguar meeting at Lubaantun. Mr. Frost's two men were hiding in the forest next to the ball court.

Mr. Frost took out his dart gun and loaded a sedative into two of the dart canisters. Placing the gun inside his hiking vest, he walked toward the noise of the kids playing.

"Be ready," he spoke into a small radio. "If any of the other kids interfere, shoot them. Shoot to kill."

Mr. Frost walked quickly in the tall grass, and soon he was next to the ball court. He slowly walked in from the north end zone. The kids quickly spotted him but kept on playing. Heather rose to her feet and kept watching, as he got closer. Soon the rubber ball was knocked in his direction, and he stopped it with his right boot.

"Greetings, kids," Mr. Frost said.

"Hi Mr. Frost," Katelynn said and walked up to retrieve the ball.

"Hi Katelynn. Where's Dr. North?" Frost asked.

"He's on the north side of the ruins complex," Katelynn said.

"That reminds us, it's time to go back to work," one of the graduate students said and retrieved his shirt. "Been fun guys, see you later," he replied and tossed the shirt to the other student and they jogged off in the morning heat.

Mr. Frost thought how his odds suddenly improved. He nodded his head and his two men appeared at the other end of the ball court and began walking toward the kids.

Chris looked right then left and felt uneasy about the situation. His instincts told him something was not right. He walked toward Katelynn and Mr. Frost.

"Ryan, go to Heather. Natalie, you too," he said quickly.

"What's wrong?" Natalie said, knowing the tone of his voice meant there was a problem.

"I'm not going with you," R.O. replied stubbornly.

"I said go stand by Heather," Chris said and turned and pointed.

At that moment, he felt a sting in the back of his neck and reached back to feel a dart. He pulled it out quickly.

"Oh my gosh," Natalie said and turned to Heather. "Run, Heather, run."

"R.O. run . . ." was all that Chris said before he fell to the ground.

Mr. Frost turned the dart gun toward R.O., pulled the trigger, and shot him with the dart in the back of his left shoulder just as he turned to run. R.O. took three steps and fell to the ground.

"Now Katelynn, you can come quietly or one of my men will shoot you with a real gun and force you anyway," Mr. Frost said.

Natalie took three big steps. Just as Frost's men were running by, she jumped and tackled one of them around the shoulders, bringing him to the ground. Chris lay unconscious. The other man grabbed R.O., tossed him over his shoulder, and started walking fast toward the helicopter.

Katelynn turned to run but Mr. Frost was too close. He grabbed her long brown hair and pulled her down from behind. While his man wrestled with Natalie, he reached inside his pocket, pulled out a syringe, and quickly injected it into Katelynn's arm as she tried to get up. In seconds she was asleep.

He tossed her over his shoulder and headed for the helicopter, only stopping for a second.

"Shoot her or I'll shoot you," he yelled at the man wrestling with Natalie.

Mr. Frost disappeared into the forest.

The man pushed Natalie away just long enough to pull a

gun from inside his jacket and point it at her. Mr. Frost was already gone.

"You move one inch and you're dead," the man said. "I don't shoot kids, but I will make an exception this time."

He started walking away, still pointing the gun at Natalie, until she turned and ran to Chris' side. He then jogged out of sight.

At the helicopter, Mr. Frost opened the second door of the small aircraft and set Katelynn down on the floor behind his seat. His accomplice laid R.O. down next to her. Within minutes, Mr. Frost was in the air and in radio contact with the *Calakmul Queen.*

"Get the *Queen* up and moving. We're going to head up the coast. Turn off all of the satellite equipment and anything that can track us from space. I'll be there in thirty minutes," Mr. Frost said.

"We got the transmission from Canada and the other one from Thompson," Emily said.

"Good. Have them ready for me. I have my cargo and we have only six days left," Mr. Frost said before he switched the radio off.

His heart was beating fast. He knew he had up to six days to carry out the ceremony, but the eclipse was only one day away. That would be the moment he would reunite with Zak Kuk.

12

Escape

Mr. Frost landed the 333 gently on the moving *Calakmul Queen* and two deck hands ran out to tie down the tiny helicopter. Opening the back storage door of the helicopter, the two men carried R.O. and Katelynn down to the lounge, where they were made comfortable on the plush couches. The drug would keep them "out" for two more hours.

Mr. Frost came in and looked at the two teens, sound asleep as if they were safe in their own beds. He then walked into his office and opened his computer. He downloaded the Dresden Codex data and immediately requested that it be cross-referenced with the Jesuit Codex. The computer was doing its magic as Mr. Frost stood and watched. Soon the last pieces of the puzzle were coming together, as each new archaeological site was matched against the three codices and the Jesuit Codex. Finally, only three lights were left on the map and the computer continued to work. Then there were two and then only one.

"I've got it," Mr. Frost said.

He picked up the satellite phone on his console and dialed a number.

"Bird Jaguar I," the voice said.

"This is Frost."

"Yes, boss?"

"Where are you?" Mr. Frost asked.

"We're about five minutes from your location. The hoist is ready for your unit and we've got all the supplies you ordered," the man said.

"Excellent," Mr. Frost said.

He picked up an intercom microphone and spoke into it.

"Bird Jaguar I ETA is twelve minutes. Prepare the pod. All hands follow the evacuation plan as directed," Mr. Frost said.

Mr. Frost then walked down to the marina deck, where the wave runners were stored, and moved over to the red Yamaha FZS. He opened the storage bin under the back seat and flipped the arming switch on the bomb that he had put there the day before, knowing that the fuel storage was just one deck below. He checked the cord that ran from the storage compartment to a laser he had mounted on the wall, hidden behind one of the many wetsuits hanging there. Mr. Frost then walked across the expansive deck to the wall where SCUBA equipment was sorted and hanging. He lifted up a buoyancy compensator vest and flipped another switch. A laser beam shot across the marina deck and reached a radio-triggering device located just above the wave runner. The beam was now activated. Whoever broke the beam would activate the bomb with ten minutes on the timer.

"That should be just enough time to get as many people on board as possible and inflict numerous casualties," Mr. Frost said. "My jaguar lord will be pleased."

Five minutes later, a big Sikorsky helicopter was hovering over the *Calakmul Queen* with its wheels barely touching the upper deck. Its weight would be too heavy for the fragile landing deck. Four men rolled Mr. Frost's environmental chamber across the deck and lifted it up inside the helicopter. Two other men were carrying R.O. and Katelynn and set them carefully on the cushion seats of the second row, buckling them in. Finally, Mr. Frost walked out with his laptop computer and one bag thrown over his shoulder. As the big helicopter took off, Kiley picked up her cell phone and dialed.

"It's me," she said. "He's gone."

"Did he tell you where he was going?" Sir Philip Patterson said.

"No, he didn't tell me; he didn't even come to look for me. I think this was supposed to be the moment of his big double cross," Kiley said.

"Well we're double-crossed if we can't follow him," Patterson said.

"Don't worry. I put the locator in the shaft of his 9 iron. He never goes anywhere without that stupid golf club," Kiley said.

"Are you sure he took it?" Patterson asked.

"I put it in the environmental chamber where he keeps it when he's off the boat," Kiley said.

"Good thinking," Patterson said.

"Now what? This boat's going to be swarming with authorities in a very short time as soon as they get a reading of where it was last anchored. We're on the move, but I've only got two hours at the most," Kiley said.

"Do you have the program?" Sir Philip asked.

"Yes, I made copies as soon as the last one came in from Thompson and the Canadians," Kiley said.

"Then get out of there quick and head for Cabo de Tres Puntas on the Guatemala coast. I'll have an amphibian there to pick you up," Sir Philip said.

"On my way," Kiley said and hung up.

She left the lounge office and watched as the crewmembers all loaded up into two Zodiac rubber boats and left the ship. Kiley went down two flights of stairs and entered the onboard marina where two wave-runners were stored along with a small, two-seat speedboat about ten feet long. Walking to the side of the speedboat, she leaned forward to pull on the deck harness and her hair just missed the laser beam. Squatting down further to jiggle the jammed apparatus, she stood up on the other side of the beam, missing it entirely. She would never know that she was almost Mr. Frost's first sacrifice.

She pushed two buttons on the deck console and the rear of the *Calakmul Queen* began to open, like a big parking garage. She disconnected all the safety ties on the speedboat and cranked the winch that lifted it off of its holding ramp. With two hands, she turned the boat around until it was facing the opening at the rear of the ship. The spring-balanced winches made it easy to lower the boat to the ejection carriage.

Suddenly, Emily and Taylor came running across the marina deck from the aft end of the yacht, having hidden during Mr. Frost's exodus.

"I was wondering if the two of you were going to make it," Kiley said.

"We were wondering that too. He has totally flipped out," Taylor said.

"Get in. We need to get out of here. He might have planted a bomb or something," Kiley said.

She retrieved her bag and computer and strapped them down in the boat. Reaching into her cotton pants pocket, she grabbed a black scrunchie and tied back her thick, red hair. She stepped into the little speedster next to Taylor and Emily. She turned the key to check the fuel and when she saw it had a full tank, she knew there was plenty of fuel for their fifteen-mile trip.

Kiley reached for the launch console, which was hanging one foot above the windshield, and pulled it down to eye level on its spring-loaded cord. She flipped a switch to the "on" position, pushed "launch" three times, and let go of the console, letting it spring up out of the way. Holding on to the wheel of the boat, Kiley heard the launch's motor underneath the boat. Within seconds a red light above her began to flash. On the third flash it turned yellow then green.

"Hang on!" she yelled.

Suddenly the carriage under the small boat began to

move rapidly and the boat was projected out of the back of the ship. Kiley pushed on the ignition switch and the in-board motor kicked on before she hit the water. The small boat surged forward at thirty miles per hour.

"Ron, I've got to tell you, you know how to plan an escape," she said to herself, as she steered into the side of a wave and leveled out.

Chris was still unconscious as Mavis, Heather, and Dr. North ran up to Natalie, who was leaning over him and crying. Heather wasn't much better.

"What happened?" Mavis yelled as she ran up.

Natalie turned and grasped her in a hug.

"They drugged him. Took Ryan and Katelynn," she sobbed. "I tried to fight one of them."

Mavis took her face in both of her hands and wiped away the blood running from Natalie's nose and from a cut over one eye.

"You gave them a good fight; I can see that," Mavis said and hugged her.

"Where did they go?" Dr. North said to Heather.

"They all left that way," Heather said, pointing toward the jungle, "through the end of the ball court. There were two goons and that Frost guy."

"Frost?" Mavis said. "What in the world would he want with our kids?"

"I don't know, but we've got to alert the authorities quick," Dr. North said, as he pulled out his cell phone and began dialing.

Mavis did the same but dialed Jack.

"Jack here," he replied.

"Honey, we've got a crisis," Mavis said.

"Talk to me," Jack said firmly.

"Frost and two men have taken Ryan and Katelynn," Mavis said as calmly as she could. Heather began to sob again.

"I wish I had done more. I just ran away," Heather said.

"Chris told you to," Natalie said.

"What? What on earth for?" Jack said, as he walked away from the group of wildlife biologists he was meeting. "I know you can't answer that."

"Dr. North is calling the authorities," Mavis said. "Jack, I just thought of something. Track down Special Agent Banister. He went with Dr. Spencer to Belmopan yesterday."

"Good idea. She'll know who to call in the government in Belize," Jack said.

"Jack. What if they are child thieves? I mean the kind of people . . ."

"Stop it, Mavis," he interrupted. "We're going to find them, and then I'll make hash out of this Frost character. What about Chris? Where was he all this time?"

"He was shot with a dart gun and drugged too. Heather ran for help and Natalie tried to fight them, but they got away," Mavis said.

"Well, Frost knew that he would have to get Chris out of the way in order to leave with the other two. Is he O.K.?" Jack asked.

"I don't know. He's sleeping now. But his breathing is normal. Dr. Craven was with Dr. North and she's attending to him," Mavis said.

"If she's there, he'll be fine. Now I'll find Special Agent Banister. You get with North and the authorities there. They couldn't go far in that little helicopter," Jack replied. "I love you. Try to be calm. We've been through this before."

"I'll be calm but you get Mickey Banister here quick," Mavis said and clicked off.

Ross Kiddie flipped the switch on his radio so he could hear it through his head set.

"Emergency message for Special Agent Banister? Yes, he's on board right now," Kiddie said into his microphone.

He looked over his shoulder and pointed to Mickey and then to his head set.

Mickey picked up the spare head set and put it on.

"Special Agent Banister, I have an emergency message for you. Hang on," Kiddie said and flipped another radio switch.

"Special Agent Banister?" the voice said.

"Yes," Mickey said into the head set.

"This is the American Consulate in Belmopan. There's been a kidnapping of an American citizen, and I have a number you should call," the woman said.

"O.K., what's the number?" Mickey replied.

A few seconds later, Ross was patching the phone call through the radio system of the helicopter.

"Hello," Mavis said, answering her phone.

"Mickey Banister, FBI, speaking," Mickey said.

"Oh, Mr. Banister, this is Mavis MacGregor and we need your help and right now," Mavis said.

"What's happened?" Mickey said.

"R.O. and Katelynn have been kidnapped by Ron Frost," Mavis said.

"I thought I felt something wrong about that guy," Mickey replied. "When and where?"

"We're in the southern range of the Maya Mountains near the ruins at Xnaheb, and it was about an hour ago, now," Mavis said. "It's a new pyramid complex called number fourteen or something."

"O.K. but let me tell you that he could be anywhere now in the little helicopter and he probably hooked up with a bigger aircraft that would take him farther and faster," Mickey replied.

"You're not making me feel better, Special Agent Banister," Mavis said.

"I know. But we've got to think with clear minds about all of our options and not follow the wrong trail. Go back to the birder camp and we'll meet you there in about an hour," Mickey said.

"I understand. We'll be there waiting," Mavis said.

"In the meantime, I can run some checks on Frost and find

out how he gets around and where he's been staying while in Belize," Mickey said. "I can also get the Belizean authorities on it and Interpol to see if Frost has a record somewhere. All of this can help us," Mickey said, feeling a lump form in his throat for R.O.

"Will do," Mavis said and hung up. Then she began to cry.

Kiley pulled up to the seaplane and the three women crawled on board, leaving the speedboat to drift off in the ocean.

"Where's Sir Philip?" she asked the pilot.

"He's waiting at the air strip at Punta Gorda, just about ten minutes away," he replied.

The ten minutes passed like a blink of the eye, and Kiley was stepping from the aircraft, which had taxied up to the marina next to an airstrip, in no time. Sir Philip walked over and took her bag, and they embraced.

"Where's the locator control?" he asked.

"In my bag," Kiley replied.

"Let's get out of this sun and then we'll check it," Patterson said. "I see you got your girls out with you. I owe them my life."

"I know, and they expect to get paid richly for it," Kiley said.

"They will be. I promise you that," Sir Philip replied.

They walked over to the edge of the airstrip and stepped up into a modern travel-trailer on wheels.

"Where'd you get this so fast?" Kiley asked.

"I rented it locally, believe it or not. Rather nice, wouldn't you say?" he replied and pulled the device out of her bag, attaching it to his lap top computer.

Within seconds, the satellite-based device was flashing on a superimposed map of the region.

"Frost only moved to Wild Cane Cay, just ten miles up the coast," Kiley said and looked up at Patterson.

"Interesting. He either doesn't know where he's going yet, or he's waiting for something," Kiley said.

"Do you have the programs?" Sir Philip asked.

"Yes, let's run them," Kiley said.

She opened her computer and entered all the codes for the codices and sat back. A few seconds later, the same series of selections that Frost had seen on his computer appeared on her screen.

"So very close all the time," Kiley said.

"He won't suspect we're coming," Sir Philip said and reached across the table, touching her hand. "Mr. Seat is readying the, shall we say, below-the-table auction on all the goods for the moment we have them. What about the law?"

"I paid two guys to sink a dive boat and strand fourteen divers off the barrier reef. That should keep them busy and delay any attempt to come south, if they even suspect what might be going on. Oh, is Seat having buyers pre-screened and requiring cash-transfers ready?" Kiley said.

"Yes, just like we planned. We just need to wait for Frost to collect the treasure before we take it away from him," Sir Philip said.

"Seat's buying a castle in Scotland for me. What's your contribution to my delinquency?" Kiley smiled.

"It's a surprise, but it'll top an old musty castle," Sir Philip replied.

The bumpy road back to the birder camp was enough to wake Chris up from the sedative and ensure he had a headache to go with it.

"Where's Ryan?" he asked first.

"Frost took him," Mavis replied as she helped him get out of the Toyota.

"Did they take Katelynn, too?" he asked, rubbing the top of his head.

"Yes, but Dad's on the phone with people who can help us, and Special Agent Banister is on his way, too," Mavis said as Natalie came up to Chris and kissed him on the cheek.

He reached out and pulled her in tight for a hug.

"And Dr. Spencer has got the Belizean National Police

involved and Interpol too," Mavis said. "She just spoke with Chief Inspector Lidia. He's sending Inspector Proctor to meet us in a seaplane."

"It happened so fast. I took two steps, and I was out like a light bulb," Chris said.

"Dr. Craven said it was a fast-acting neurotoxin, just enough not to kill you. It's that strong," Natalie said as they led him into Jack and Mavis' bungalow.

"Here's a glass of cold water, Chris," Heather said walking up. "Dr. Craven said you need to drink lots of water to get the toxin out of your system."

"Thanks Heather," Chris said and took the glass. "And hey, you did what I told you to do. What if all of us had been drugged? No one would be around to tell the story. And what happened to your face?" Chris said, just noticing Natalie's cuts and bruises for the first time.

"She gave that guy a heck of a time, kicking, hitting, and biting," Heather said.

"You did? He could have shot you or stabbed you!" Chris said.

"He didn't, and I'm here to prove it," Natalie said and smiled.

"She was very brave today," Mavis said, trying to remain calm.

Jack walked in, sat down on the small couch, and leaned back. He looked frustrated.

"What's wrong?" Mavis asked nervously.

Jack got back up and unsnapped the utility belt he wore when hiking on their adventures. He flung it across the room and spun on his heels.

"When I catch up with Frost, he is going to wish he were dead!"

At that moment, Mr. Frost sat quietly in his environmental chamber, cooling down as the helicopter flew up the coast. He again wondered who he would sacrifice first: Ryan or Katelynn?

13

The *Calakmul Queen*

"This is Banister speaking," Mickey spoke into the headset from his seat in the back of the helicopter.

"A ship on the Caribbean headed north? Yes, I can be there. We're just about to land and pick up the MacGregors to bring with us. Weapons? Well, you don't really want me to answer that, do you?" Mickey said. "O.K., we'll radio back for coordinates."

"Sergeant Major Kiddie, you wouldn't happen to have extra weapons on board would you?" Mickey asked.

Kiddie reached back and handed him a set of keys.

"Open the compartment behind your seat," Kiddie said and smiled.

Mickey and Kim stood up and folded the seat down. Mickey unlocked the compartment and pulled the front forward. They looked at each other and raised their eyebrows at the same time. Placed securely in racks were two Colt M16 automatic rifles, two Colt .45 semi-automatic pistols, a Smith & Wesson .357, a Ruger Super Redhawk .44 Magnum, and two flare guns. Lining the bottom of the case was enough ammunition to hold off a small army for a few hours.

"Sergeant Major, I am impressed but not surprised. Mind if I borrow your Ruger and one of the rifles?" Mickey asked.

"I'd be honored Special Agent," Kiddie said and smiled. "One requirement though."

"What's that?" Mickey answered.

"You put one of those .44s right between the eyes of that Frost character. Anyone who kidnaps children should receive no mercy," he said.

"Could I borrow one of the small guns in case we get shot at?" Kim said shyly.

"Help yourself," Kiddie replied.

Mickey handed her a .45 caliber pistol just before the helicopter landed to pick up the MacGregors.

"Let me show you how to load it," Mickey said.

"You forget, I'm from Texas too," Kim said as she popped the clip, checked the rounds, shoved it back in, loaded a round in the chamber, and clicked on the safety. "I'm ready."

Within minutes, the MacGregor clan and Natalie were aboard and their adrenaline was still running high. Mickey showed the gun stash to Jack and Chris and they each loaded up with weapons and ammunition.

"I've got the coordinates of Frost's ship. It's moving northeast, away from the coast. Inspector Proctor won't get here for two more hours, but we can be there in twenty minutes on this helicopter," Mickey said.

"Then let's go for it," Jack said and checked the clip in the Colt .45. "We may be the only hope those kids have." He tried to swallow, but his emotions were elevated.

"My sentiments exactly," Mickey answered.

The twenty minutes flew by quickly and Ross Kiddie sounded off the distance as they drew closer.

"Ship dead ahead!"

He swung the Aérospatiale behind the ship and started to come in low. Jack opened the side door. As soon as Ross had the helicopter two feet off the upper deck, Jack, Chris, and Mickey bailed out, brandishing their weapons and hugging the deck as Ross banked the chopper for a fast retreat, the rotary blades coming five feet off the deck and just missing the Schweizer 333.

Chris moved to the stairs first and carefully made it to the bridge the next deck down. Jack went down the starboard side while Mickey worked his way aft. Going slow, not knowing how many people they might meet, each man took maximum precaution to avoid a gun battle because the two kids might be on board. After ten minutes, Chris and Jack finally met up in the large lounge and looked at each other in surprise.

Mickey walked in from a side hallway.

"Looks abandoned to me," he said.

"Same here," Jack said.

Chris took out his phone and called Mavis, who was still in the helicopter.

"The ship is abandoned," he said.

"Oh my," Mavis said. "I was afraid of that when we didn't see or hear anything right away."

"We'll get back to you in a minute. I might fly the 333 out of the way and let Ross land on the upper deck. It can support that size helicopter," Chris said.

"O.K., we'll wait to hear from you," Mavis said.

"Well let's go up and try it," Chris said.

All three men got to the upper deck and Chris stated the obvious.

"Where did I think I would fly this thing?" he said.

"I don't know; I was just going along with you," Mickey said.

"Let's push it overboard so Ross can land," Jack said.

"Good idea, Dad," Chris said and slung the rifle over his shoulder.

Within minutes the 333 was bobbing on the ocean waves and soon to be a new artificial reef.

Kiddie landed the helicopter without a problem and the girls stepped off. Everyone fanned out around the ship looking for clues and soon met back in the lounge.

"Nothing," Jack said.

"All I saw was a little flashing light above the red wave runner," Heather said.

"That's sounds weird. I better check," Mickey said. "Could be an alarm system."

"I'll go with you," Chris said. "Dad, start going through the computer to see if you can find something."

Chris and Mickey were soon on the marina deck and approaching the wave runners when Mickey suddenly stopped. He reached out and moved a wet suit on the wall a couple of inches with the barrel of his gun.

"That's an alarm alright. It's a laser beam. Heather must have set off a timer," Mickey said as he got close to the wave runner and lifted the lid to the storage compartment. "No alarm. It's a bomb. Looks like C-4 or Semtex. And enough to blow four of these yachts to pieces."

"What'll we do?" Chris said.

"The timer says two minutes and counting," Mickey said and sat down next to the explosives.

He carefully checked all the wires leading from the timer mechanism to the plastic explosives. He found blasting caps at the end of the wires and pressed securely into the Semtex.

"I need your help. There's not enough time to get off the ship. We would clear the blast zone, but the explosion would blind you and blow your ears out and the fish would still eat you," Mickey said.

"Hold this red wire while I follow the yellow one," he said.

"Got it," Chris replied.

"O.K., now hold the yellow one, too, while I follow the blue one," Mickey said.

"The timer says one minute," Chris said.

"Didn't your mother teach you that clocks don't tell time, they read time?" Mickey said softly.

"What?" Chris said.

"Just passing the time while I pull on the black one," Mickey said.

"Thirty seconds," Chris said nervously. "Are you sure you can do that?"

"No, but it's the only one I can't trace, so it's got to be the lead or something," Mickey said.

"Or what?" Chris asked as he watched the clock near zero. "What about the green one?"

"I didn't see that one," Mickey said and grimaced.

"Oh my gosh," Chris said softly.

"Back to the black one. I don't know where it leads to, but here it is," Mickey smiled and pulled out the black wire just as the timer reached zero.

"Kaboom!" Mickey shouted.

"That's not funny," Chris said and stood up.

"Son, if you don't get a sense of humor, you will die early for sure," Mickey said and pulled the entire explosive wiring free. "That was too easy. They didn't expect anyone to find it, and they wanted to sink the ship. I'm guessing we're standing over the fuel tanks. He must have wanted someone else to die, because he sure didn't know we'd be aboard, raiding his kitchen."

"It would have made a huge explosion," Chris said. "Maybe he wanted to cover his exit."

Mickey and Chris went back up to the lounge and showed everyone the makeshift bomb that Mr. Frost had left behind.

"Heather, you tripped the laser beam when you were down there and triggered the timing switch," Chris said.

"My luck I guess," she said.

"I can't get in the computer. I don't know his password," Natalie said.

"Does anyone have anything about the Mayans? His password is probably related to something Mayan," Kim said.

"I have a book in my pack that we were using for the ball court," Heather said.

"Go get it and quick," Jack said.

Within minutes, Heather was back and gave the book to Mavis.

"Look up the name for the *Calakmul Queen,*" Mickey said.

Mavis thumbed through the volume quickly, checking the index first.

"Here it is, page 457," Mavis said.

"The only known female queen to have succeeded her husband the king was Zak Kuk of Calakmul. That's Z-a-k K-u-k."

"Zak Kuk," Natalie said out loud as she typed it into the computer. "Bingo!" she yelled.

Everyone rushed to the computer as she started opening files.

"Good job, Special Agent," Jack said to Banister.

"Just call me Mickey like the little fella' does," he answered.

"There are listings for four different Mayan codices," Natalie said. "Also a cross-referencing program of some kind."

Natalie continued to type and look at files until the computer screen started to light up and pictures and calculations appeared.

"Wow, would you look at that?" Jack said.

"My guess is that he found a way to find the tombs of the lost kings of the Maya," Kim said. "I thought that a key was in existence somewhere, but we didn't know where to look. It was only speculation that the kings may have bonded together in the last days to oppose the Spanish invaders."

"Look at this," Mavis said as she stood behind them, holding the Jesuit Codex.

Kim walked over to it, took it, and set it down. Opening it slowly she gasped.

"Archaeologists didn't know this codex even existed," she said as she carefully turned the pages. "Here is a list of the lost kings of the forest. Amazing! The post-Columbian retreat from the Spanish. Plans to revolt. They were planning to garner all their forces against the invaders and drive them out. Frost must be the one who's been looting the temples we didn't know about. He must have a warehouse full of artifacts and treasure."

"Put a price tag on it, doc," Mickey said.

"It's priceless. To underworld collectors, you're looking at $400 million at the least."

"But this boat is worth millions. Why would he want to destroy it just to have something else?" Heather said.

"Because he's insane," Mickey said. "And he can buy twenty of these boats with all the loot he's stolen."

"Hey everyone, look at this," Jack said, standing over a chrome-and-steel trunk. "He left in a hurry and forgot something."

"Stand back please," Mickey said and pulled the trigger on the .44 Magnum, blasting the lock right off and tearing a gash in the front side of the trunk.

"Glad we weren't over the fuel tanks," Chris said and smiled.

"I thought about that before I fired," Mickey said and smiled.

Kim opened the trunk and pulled out the jade and gold masks quickly.

"I'm amazed. These are worth millions," she said. "It looks like there were three or four masks, but only these two are left. And here's a fragment of a jaguar skin."

"And what's this?" Mickey said, as he held up a feather.

"It's a feather from a quetzal bird, a sacred animal," Kim said.

"Is that blood on it?" Mickey asked. He walked out on the deck to look at the feather in the sunlight and noticed the blood stain on the teak wood for the first time. He walked around spotting wax drippings from the candles, and then he looked out to sea and braced himself.

The others came out of the lounge and noticed his strange posture.

"What's wrong?" Mavis asked, her motherly instinct surfacing.

Mickey turned around and looked everyone in the eye one by one before he spoke.

"Frost is an insane sociopath, probably a psychopath. All around us are candle drippings, blood stains on the deck, part of a jaguar skin, and quetzal feathers, things that I think would only be associated with the royalty of the Maya. I think he believes he is the reincarnate king of the Maya and his mother is Zak Kuk.," he said.

"Oh no!," gasped Heather from the end of the deck, behind Mickey, putting her hands over her mouth.

"What's wrong, sweets?" Mavis said and hurried over to her.

"Look," she said and pointed to the deck, indicating the smudged out letters of "Ryan" and "Katelynn."

"Jack! Their names are written in blood on the deck," Mavis shouted in despair.

"That only means he was planning it here," Mickey said.

"Planning what?" Heather asked quietly, suspecting the answer.

"Ryan and Katelynn are his human sacrifices so he can turn into a Mayan King," Kim said. "I'm sorry."

"Someone had to say it, but that doesn't mean it has to happen. Natalie, go check the computer," Jack said forcefully and hugged Mavis.

Everyone stood still for several minutes, staring at the names in dried blood.

There was a yell in the lounge, and Natalie came running out on to the deck.

"I've got it. He's going to Wild Cane Cay!" Natalie said. "All the coordinates from the codex point to one spot on the entire Belizean coast, Wild Cane Cay."

"Chris, you're flying us there now in the *Raptor*. We'll have Mr. Kiddie follow in the *Calakmul Queen*. Kim, you're coming with us in case we need to follow any clues written in Maya hieroglyphs. Special Agent Banister, pack all the heat you can find off this boat. Now let's get moving before Frost can hurt those kids," Jack ordered.

As Chris familiarized himself with the console of the helicopter, Mickey located the ship's armory and stocked up on more weapons and ammunition. Jack went down to the marina to look for more bombs and then returned to the flight deck. Soon they were loading into the helicopter. Kiddie walked out and opened Chris' door.

"Take care of her son. She's a fine whirly bird," Ross said and shook his hand. "Never thought I would be in the Navy," he laughed and went down one flight of stairs to the bridge of the ship.

"Where's Heather?" Jack asked as Mavis climbed aboard.

"She's staying with Mr. Kiddie," Mavis replied.

"Good idea," Jack said and pulled Mavis inside the chopper. "Let's go!"

The blue and silver helicopter lifted off and headed north toward Wild Cane Cay. They all hoped they were in time to stop a tradition the Mayans had done for centuries: the sacrifice of two innocent children.

14

Blood Cave

"My dad is going to rip your head off and feed it to pigs," yelled R.O. as one of Mr. Frost's assistants pulled the tape off his mouth. R.O. had been faking an asthma attack, and the men thought he needed more air. "Then he'll pull your arms off and throw them to the sharks."

"Put the tape back on the brat," Mr. Frost said impatiently.

"How much further boss?" the helicopter pilot asked.

"About five minutes at these same coordinates, then start looking for a landing zone."

A few minutes later the helicopter was setting down in an opening so small that the rotary blades trimed some leaves off the trees. There were five men with Mr. Frost and each had an assigned duty of carrying equipment. Soon they were walking single file through the jungle about two hundred yards from the beach.

Mr. Frost kept consulting his computer and GIS equipment, adjusting their path by a few feet every so often. R.O. and Katelynn cooperated because they knew they would be dragged through the forest. R.O. thought Mr. Frost's men seemed to obey every order without question, like zombies.

"O.K., we're going downhill, so watch your step," Mr. Frost yelled out.

Suddenly Mr. Frost stopped and looked around. He felt as if someone was watching. Shaking his head, he decided to move onward. After they had traveled about a quarter of mile through the rainforest, Mr. Frost stopped.

"It's got to be right here," he said out loud.

"Boss, I don't see nothing," one of his men said.

Mr. Frost reached over and pulled his 9-iron from his pack. He grabbed the club by the head and started using it as a walking stick and to push branches out of his way.

"Come in front of me and walk straight toward that big tree," he commanded to one of his men.

"Sure boss," the man replied.

The man was a giant of a brute and was a good bodyguard, which is why Mr. Frost hired him in the first place. His men knew that after one year of service they would receive $1 million each and be released to do anything they desired.

The man looked at the tree about fifty feet away and walked directly toward it. He hadn't gone twenty steps when suddenly he disappeared, as if he were sucked into the bowels of the earth. Two of the men called out his name, but Mr. Frost just stood there. R.O. and Katelynn were shocked but remained quiet.

"Just as I thought," Mr. Frost said.

He then walked over to the spot where the assistant had fallen and pulled back some of the foliage to reveal a perfectly designed hole in the ground cut out of solid rock. Turning back to the group he barked, "Stay here and don't move."

Mr. Frost sat down next to the hole then slid carefully into the hole on his back until he felt some steps. He pulled out a flashlight and turned it on. He bent over and started walking downward. He found his man about ten feet down, alive and still surprised, with just a bump on his head.

"Get up. You'll live," he said.

The man grunted a few words and got up.

"Now, go back up and bring everyone down here," Mr. Frost said and shined his flashlight on the stairs so the man could see his way out.

He began to move farther downward as soon as he could hear everyone filing into the cave, one by one, with flashlights pointing in all directions. Mr. Frost stayed fifty feet ahead of the group and soon entered a larger cavern. Bones were scattered seemingly everywhere and a pile of children's skulls were stacked ten feet high against one wall. There must have been three hundred or more.

"Look," Katelynn said and pointed to the skulls.

R.O. looked at the skulls and then looked at Mr. Frost but stopped before saying what was on his mind. He knew he would get a slap or kick in the face.

The group walked for twenty minutes through a labyrinth of caves until they could begin to smell the sea. As they entered a large cavern, they came to a pool of water in the middle about thirty feet across. Human bones were everywhere. Mr. Frost walked over to the water, leaned down, touched it, and tasted it.

"Sea water. This cave must be connected to the ocean by a long tunnel," he said and stood up.

He walked over to a large rock, which had been flattened and had dark stains all over it.

"A sacrificial stone," he said reverently.

"Boss, look," one of his men said, standing next to the pool of water. "There's an opening to another room through the water. Must be a low tide opening."

"Go find it," Mr. Frost said. The man jumped into the water and swam across the pool until the opening was just below him on the side of the cave. He took a deep breath and went down into the hole, holding a flashlight in one hand. The light disappeared.

Several minutes passed and the man returned. As he broke free above the water, he said "You won't believe it boss."

Mr. Frost dropped his pack and dove into the water to go

through the hole. Five minutes later he was back.

"Everyone in the water and through. Cut the kids' hands free so they can swim. If they disobey, break an arm but don't kill them," he said.

Katelynn shivered at the thought.

Soon the entire group was in the water, with all the equipment and packs, swimming into the next chamber.

R.O. climbed out of the water and walked over to a pile of pottery and debris. He picked up a solid-gold headdress helmet and put it on.

"Wow, it's beautiful," Katelynn said, as she walked over next to him.

Scattered all over the cave amid human bones were gold jewelry, jade bracelets and necklaces, obsidian pieces of all kinds, and hundreds of pieces of painted pottery.

"This is it! This is the main treasure hold of the Mayan kings," Mr. Frost said.

"Boss, you should see the next room. It's even more packed than this one," the guard said.

Mr. Frost was standing next to a cave wall, reading the hieroglyphs.

"This says that the kings brought their gold and riches here to escape the Spanish, then they killed themselves as a sacrifice to the gods," he said and turned around.

"Tie the children's hands and feet. I need to rest," he said and sat down on a rock, leaning back into the cave wall.

The French-made Aérospatiale Dauphin banked sharply to the south and circled the small island off the southern coast of Belize. Special Agent Banister was sitting in the copilot's seat with Jack just behind him. They flew across the island from a high altitude before diving down to treetop level.

"Natalie, are you sure about those coordinates?" Jack asked.

"Yes, I'm pretty sure this is the place," she replied.

Jack took the laptop computer and began to re-run all the numbers from the Jesuit Codex.

"Chris, find a place to set down so we can conserve fuel," Special Agent Banister said.

"Gotcha. There's a field down there next to the beach," Chris replied.

The helicopter came to a hover just over the clearing as Chris rotated it completely around, looking for any problems that could arise on their landing. In a few seconds, the helicopter settled firmly on the grass.

Just as Kim stepped out of the helicopter, a smaller Hughes 500 helicopter flew directly overhead and Kiley Spencer looked down.

"Oh, my gosh. There's Kim," Kiley said and immediately turned to look at David Seat.

"I thought you said she was showing some old FBI guy around Belize," Seat said.

"She was. Maybe she still is," Kiley said. "That looked like a large group of people. But it was also one of the *Barrier Reef Tours* helicopters," Kiley replied. "They do a big charter business from here to Cancun. That one was the *Raptor.* Can't miss Ross Kiddie's big dinosaur on the side."

"Well, she's off-track if she's following Frost," Seat said.

"You're right. The GPS has Frost just one mile inland across from the cay. That's only three miles, but it's enough to make you miss if you're using only the codex," Kiley said.

"If it's more than three hundred yards in this jungle, it might as well be three hundred miles," Seat replied.

"Where's Sir Philip?" Kiley asked realizing that she had come ashore, hopped on the helicopter, and not even thought about his presence or lack of contact.

"He's presently on a fast-moving ship loaded with all the equipment we'll need to salvage the lost treasure of the Mayan kings. We estimated that we would need heavy trucks, a small crane, and a hovercraft to ferry the goods from the rainforest to the ship," Seat replied.

"You think of everything," Kiley said.

"I had to front the captain of the ship $500,000 to guarantee all the equipment would be on board," Seat said with a frown on his face.

"Was that the $500,000 you beat me out of?" Kiley asked and smiled.

"I don't know where I went wrong!" Natalie said with desperation in her voice.

"That's alright honey," Mavis replied and touched her shoulder.

The corners of Natalie's mouth turned down and tears formed in her eyes. Chris walked around the helicopter, making a visual check of the systems. Mickey, Kim, and Jack kept going over the coordinates, assuming that the Jesuit Codex was the master program and the Dresden, Madrid, and Paris codices were the application. They kept coming up with Wild Cane Cay as the primary coordinate.

"How far are we from the mainland?" Mickey asked.

"About two miles," Kim replied and adjusted her sunglasses.

"The most we could be off is 1.5 miles," Mickey said and stood up, dusting the dirt off his pants from the old tree trunk on which they had been sitting.

"That's not much but if we are off one and a half miles, then that puts the treasure chamber in the middle of the water," Jack said.

"In the middle of the water . . . hmm. That gets my brain spinning. A few years ago some archaeologists discovered that a cenote in the Yucatan connected to the ocean through an underground cave system and that it opened nearly 1,200 feet from the shore line," Kim said.

"But that would mean this cave, if there is such a cave, would be three or four times that length," Jack said.

"The Mayans didn't have SCUBA and couldn't travel that distance underwater," Chris said as he walked up.

"Yes, but the cave system wouldn't have to be underwater all the way, just part of the way," Jack replied.

"But if there were any ridges or plates in this area, then the sea floor would be closer to the surface," Mickey said.

Jack pulled his telephone out of his pocket and dialed a series of numbers. There was a long pause before he heard a ring. On the third ring someone picked up.

"Jim, here," trader Jim said from Kodiak, Alaska, where he owns a large lodge as a cover for his position as an undercover CIA operative watching the international fishing grounds off the Alaskan coast.

"Jim, this is Jack," Jack replied.

"Hey buddy, how's those kids and that pretty wife of yours?" Jim asked in his normal jovial tone.

"Got a problem, Jim. Seems a sociopath millionaire who wants to be king of the Mayans has taken Ryan to sacrifice to his gods," Jack said quickly, not wanting to say the words or hear them.

"Now hold on a minute. Who is this madman?" Jim asked.

"His name is Ron Frost," Jack replied.

"Give me a minute," Jim said.

Trader Jim was back on the phone within two minutes.

"He has no record of any kind. Just an eccentric artifact collector," Jim said.

"Can you bring up on your computer any information about the seafloor in the Gulf of Honduras?" Jack asked.

"Sure can. Give me the coordinates," Jim replied.

"Sixteen degrees, thirty-one minutes north by eighty-eight degrees, seventy-two minutes west," Jack read from his map.

"O.K., give me a minute," Jim said.

There was a forty-five second pause before Trader Jim came back on the line.

"Looks like there are two ridges in that part of the Gulf of Honduras. One runs north and south from Punta Gorda, Belize, to Livingston, Guatemala. The other runs east and west from the shore south of Punta Negra, Belize, to the barrier reef and further out into the Gulf," Jim said.

"That's got to be it," Jack said.

"It what?" Jim asked.

"We thought we had the exact coordinates, but they dropped us right in the middle of the ocean. Then our resident archaeologist said it might be a cave complex that runs ashore," Jack said, sounding frustrated.

"How can I help?" Jim asked.

"I don't know, really I don't," Jack replied.

"I will sit by the phone until I hear that Ryan is safe. If you need satellite help, let me know and I'll set one of those birds right over you," Jim said.

"I won't ask how you do that, but I will remember," Jack said.

"Take care and give my love to Mavis," Jim said.

"Thanks, Jim," Jack said and hung up.

Trader Jim Gailey got up from his desk and pulled the horn on a ram's-head trophy hanging on the wall. The secret wall moved just enough for him to slide through to the hidden room. He sat down at another console and put on a headset. After punching in some numbers a voice appeared on the line.

"Go ahead," it said.

"Wolf bait niner niner zero niner," Jim said.

"Line secure," the voice said.

"Request urgent information about one Ron Frost," Jim said.

"Will reply," the voice said and the line was broken.

Jim returned to his desk and looked out across the expanse of Kodiak Island through his giant picture window. He wished he was in Central America to help his friends, the MacGregors.

15

Dr. Lamb

Ross Kiddie piloted the *Calakmul Queen* to within three hundred yards of Wild Cane Cay before he picked up the radio.

"*Calakmul Queen* to *Raptor,*" he said as he keyed the mike.

"That sounds like the Sergeant Major," Kim said from the shade of the helicopter.

"It sure is," Mickey said and walked over to the radio in the helicopter.

"Special Agent Banister here," Mickey said.

"Well, I've got this old tub about three hundred yards off the south side of the cay. Any news?" Kiddie asked.

"Not much as of yet," Mickey said. "I think we're all coming back to see you in about ten minutes, so go ahead and drop anchor."

"Will do. We'll be waiting," he said and smiled at Heather who was sitting in the bridge compartment.

Despite Mavis's objections, everyone climbed back into the helicopter and Chris lifted off for the two-minute flight to the ship. Mavis didn't want to leave the island, because she was clinging to anything that might lead them to Ryan and Katelynn. When the helicopter landed on the top deck,

Heather was waiting by the stairs. She hugged her mom and they walked together down to the lounge where everyone decided to regroup, except for Chris. He went down to the marina deck again and a few minutes later he was back in the lounge.

"Hey everybody, I'm going to take one of the wave runners and ride it up to the beach, along where Trader Jim said the ridge was," he said.

"You can't go alone," Mavis said.

"I'll go," Jack said immediately.

"Better let me go, Dr. MacGregor," Mickey said. "We need someone here to coordinate anything that the authorities might do when they arrive."

"But it will be dark in two more hours," Kim said.

"We'll be back, and we can take a sandwich or something," Mickey said.

"I'll go to the kitchen and see if I can find something for you to take to eat," Natalie volunteered and hurried off.

As Chris and Mickey worked on their plans, Natalie found a tube of salami and a box of crackers. She grabbed a case of bottled water and lugged it up the stairs to the lounge. On the second trip, she brought the food.

"I should have helped," Mavis said as she saw her with the load.

"I got it just fine," Natalie said.

"Now, Chris and I are going to do this and look around, which means we may not come back before dark," Mickey said. "I don't want anyone to panic and come look for us and make a lot of noise. It might tip off Frost and his bunch if they're in there. You can contact us on our radio."

"Just be careful," Mavis said and hugged Chris. He had already slung an M16 rifle across his back and holstered a Colt .45 semi-automatic pistol.

Mickey grabbed another rifle and a bag with half the provisions. Jack and Kim picked up the rest and followed Chris and Mickey down to the marina deck. Chris found the hanging console and opened the rear, bay entrance to the ship. He then flipped the switch that activated the mini-crane, which lowered the waver runner into the water. Jack stuffed the food and water into the storage compartment—the same one that had held the bomb. With a quick wave, Chris and Mickey were off, out the rear of the ship, and Jack closed the large door that sealed off the ocean.

The sun was still high off the horizon as Chris and Mickey cleared the end of the island and headed for the beach two miles away. The lush green of the jungle was breathtaking in its beauty, and both men wondered about their mission and if Ryan and Katelynn were still alive. As they neared the coast, Chris slowed down and looked for a wave to ride to the beach. He spotted one.

"Hang on," he yelled to Mickey, who was holding down his hat.

"I'm with ya!" Mickey replied and adjusted his hat, rifle, and pistol: the three things he needed most.

The wave runner cruised along a crest of a large wave and then Chris gunned it and fell into the trough for the ride to the beach. When he felt the sand dig into the bottom of the craft, Chris turned off the motor. They both got off and dragged the heavy machine as far as they could out of the water.

Suddenly, they heard a squeal and turned around. There was a child about eight years old standing at the tree line with a small pig in his arms. Three other pigs of varying sizes were standing around his feet. He just stared at Mickey and Chris.

"*Hola,*" Mickey said.

The child didn't move.

"Maybe he doesn't speak Spanish," Chris said.

"You're probably right on this one. These modern Maya still have about a dozen different dialects. But 'hello' shouldn't have changed that much," Mickey said.

Suddenly the boy turned and ran back into the forest with the pigs running right behind him.

"Did you see that?" Chris said.

"Sure did. I heard pigs were smarter than horses," Mickey said.

"But we don't eat horses," Chris said.

"Can't be too smart, can they?" Mickey said.

"Let's follow," Chris said and started to walk toward the trees.

"Better take some water," Mickey said and handed two bottles to Chris who stuck them in the satchel hanging from his shoulder, which was holding extra clips for the rifles and pistols.

Within a minute, the two men were on the trail of the boy and the pigs. Luckily for them, the pigs were trampling down the foliage as they raced through the forest, leaving a clear trail to follow. The trail was level for quite some time before it started to climb.

"We must have reached the edge of those hills we could see from the boat," Mickey said. "I should have cut back on the chocolate malts when I thought I was going to retire."

"This elevation isn't too bad. Reminds me of the mountains of New Guinea," Chris said.

"Your family does get around," Mickey said and stopped to wipe the sweat off his forehead. He took off his hat and wiped his whole face.

Chris stopped and sat down on a fallen tree. He was startled by a sudden screeching noise, resembling a cat in pain. Chris jumped up and pulled the Colt .45 out of the holster.

"Don't worry. It's just a kinkajou," Mickey said.

"A kinkajou?" Chris said.

"It resembles a big cat. Throw in a teddy bear, and the agility of a monkey with big teeth, and you've got a kinkajou," Mickey said.

"Where did you learn that?" Chris smiled.

"That cute red head, Dr. Kim, told me just yesterday," Mickey said.

"She is cute but twenty years closer to my age than yours," Chris laughed.

"You better not let Miss Natalie hear you say that," Mickey said.

"You're exactly right about that," Chris agreed.

"Better get moving before we lose all light. I don't think we're going to make it back to the beach tonight," Mickey said and picked up his rifle. "I don't think we will find that boy and the pigs, but let's see where this trail leads."

Back on the trail, they walked up hill for nearly an hour, as darkness crept into the forest and drops of rain found their way through the canopy down to the trail. No longer able to see the trail, Mickey took out the one light they had packed and led the way, still following the crushed foliage. As they forged along, every insect that detected these 100-degree heated bodies passing by made a mad leap to hitch a ride, causing great irritation to Chris and Mickey.

They heard a generator echoing through the rainforest. Both men stopped and looked at each other.

"Did you hear that?" Chris asked.

"Sure did," Mickey replied. "Must be a village up ahead."

Within five minutes they could see light and hear a gasoline generator running. Crossing through a clearing, they reached the edge of a village of twenty five to thirty small houses. At the edge of the village stood four men, dressed in clothes obviously given to them by a church group or other organization from somewhere in the United States. The style and colors were not common for the plazas that Mickey or Chris had seen in Guatemala or Belize.

The men didn't run or seem alarmed as Chris and Mickey walked up.

"Hola," Mickey tried again.

"Hello," said a voice from behind the the four men.

A man about five feet, nine inches tall with brown hair down to his collar and a full beard came into view. He wore khaki shorts and shirt and leather sandals.

"Americans?" the man asked, and adjusted his glasses.

"Yes, we are. Mickey Banister, special agent, FBI. This is

Chris MacGregor," Mickey said and walked closer with his right hand on the grip of the M16, ready to pull it up and use it if necessary. Chris had slid his rifle off his shoulder, as well.

"What's the FBI doing in the Maya Mountains of Belize?" the man asked.

"We're following the trail of kidnappers," Mickey said cautiously.

"Kidnappers. That's amazing. It sounds like a movie plot or something," the man said.

"No movie, but it's a serious plot for sure," Mickey said as a couple drops of water rolled off the brim of his Panama hat. "We ran into a small boy on the beach and followed him."

"That was a boy from the next village north. He had a sick pig and brought it to me to check over," the man said.

"You're a pig doctor?" Mickey said.

"Well, sort of," the man said. "Have you eaten anything?"

"Not yet. We brought a few rations but didn't stop because we thought we might lose the boy's trail through the rainforest," Chris said.

"Well, why don't you join me?" the man said. "I don't get that many visitors down here. I forgot to introduce myself. I'm Dr. Lamb."

"So you are a doctor?" Chris said.

"Yes, but not what you think," he said.

Chris and Mickey stayed close behind Lamb as he walked through the village. The steady hum of the generator grew louder until they finally stopped at a house that had a corral full of animals, some bandaged and ailing. The small Honda generator was quietly humming on the side of the house and was connected to a large metal barrel full of fuel.

As Lamb entered the house, Chris and Mickey stepped up from the dirt of the pathway to a wooden floor. They both looked down in surprise at the same time.

"Oh, I couldn't get used to the dirt floors so I built a wooden floor. There's a latrine out back and I have fans in every room. Since there are only three rooms, it wasn't a big deal," Lamb said.

He spoke to a Mayan lady in a dialect that neither Mickey nor Chris had never heard before and turned to his guests.

"This is my cook and housekeeper. She and her husband live next door. She will fix us some lamb, black beans, and fresh tortillas," Lamb said.

Chris turned and walked into the next room, which was well lit. Medical supplies were stacked all around and equipment of all kinds was piled on three different tables. He walked back to the main room.

"Are you a medical doctor or a veterinarian?" Chris asked.

"Neither. I'm an oral surgeon," Lamb replied.

"An oral surgeon?" Mickey said.

"Yes and when I'm needed to fix something else, either belonging to a human or a pig, I try to do what I can," Lamb said. "Sit down, please."

The three sat around a table that had a high polish on it.

"We have a situation where a psychopath has kidnapped two children and is going to sacrifice them in an old Mayan ceremony. This guy thinks he will become the new King of the Mayans," Mickey said.

"That's terrible," Lamb replied. "We haven't had any unusual disturbances lately. I have learned from the people of the area about all of the myths concerning the last days of the Mayans and the stories about the kings walking through the jungles loaded down with treasure to hide from the Spanish. But it's all local myth and superstition. In fact, the locals are getting ready for one of their celebrations, set for tomorrow afternoon," Lamb said.

"Tomorrow? What is it?" Chris asked.

"There's a solar eclipse at 3:33 tomorrow afternoon," Lamb replied.

"That's it!," Mickey said with fire in his eyes. "Frost will enact the ceremony at 3:33 and sacrifice the kids then."

"How do the people know these things? I mean, there

obviously isn't much education around here," Chris said.

"Now, don't pass judgment on them just because you don't see a brick school building or library. They have serious traditions and are very religious. There are men in the village who keep track of time, the movement of the moon and sun, and who watch other heavenly bodies. Their fathers did this before them and their fathers before them. Most believe the skill was passed down since the beginning of the Long Count," Lamb said.

"The Long Count. There it is again," Mickey said.

"Tell me more about the myths," Chris said. "Are there any unreported ruins in the region? I mean, some the villagers know about but won't tell the archaeologists who come through?"

"Well, yes, there are. But I can't tell you that. It might hurt their way of life if those locations were cleaned up and promoted for tourism. I don't know that the village would get any of the money anyway," Lamb said.

"What if our guy, Frost, was going to perform the ceremony at the old ruins nearby, and the lives of these two kids were at stake," Mickey said looking him in the eye.

"Then I would take you to them at the first light of day," Lamb said.

"Why not now?" Chris asked.

Lamb thought for a minute and seemed to come to a decision.

"Let's eat so we have enough energy to get there. I'll go down the road and get the best tracker in the region," Lamb replied, and got up and left the house.

Mickey took out the radio he had brought from the ship.

"Banister to *Calakmul Queen,*" he said.

"Jack here. Go ahead Mickey."

"We've got a lead. We'll be in the jungle all night. Stay by the radio," Mickey said.

"Will do, be safe," Jack said and turned to Mavis.

"You heard?" Jack asked.

"Yes, but I . . ." She started crying and then caught herself and took a deep breath. "I hope they take Frost alive, because I want just ten minutes with him alone," Mavis said heatedly and narrowed her eyes.

"I know, honey, me too," Jack said.

16

Maya Blue

Two hours earlier, archaeologist Dr. Kiley Spencer and international financier-banker David Seat had pinpointed the homing device hidden in Frost's nine-iron, locating it just one hour before sunset. They crisscrossed the rainforest canopy at a high altitude to ensure they would not alert Frost and his gang of bodyguards. Totally unaware of the kidnapping of Ryan MacGregor and Katelynn Komarovski, they were simply waiting until the treasure was removed from its lair and brought to the surface. They had no intention of doing any of the dirty work.

"Yes, Sir Philip. We know where it is and we are waiting for Frost to bring it to us. Then we'll eliminate him and bring it to you," Seat said into the satellite phone. "Yes, I have bankers on four continents ready to make the transactions during the private auction. Yes, my estimate is half a billion at least, not counting the pieces you want for your private collection or finding Frost's warehouse where he is hiding his collection. That could bring another $100 million, easily. Yes, she's here."

Seat handed the telephone to Kiley.

"Hi love," Kiley said. "We've just about got it. No, Kim

won't be a problem. No worries there. I'll simply offer her a million dollars to keep quiet, and I'm sure she'll do it. I said *no problems,* so drop it."

Kiley let out a deep sigh and handed the phone back to Seat who then ended the conversation.

"I don't know why he does that," Kiley said.

"He's as paranoid as Frost is. Anyone who collects at that level has to be. Artifacts like these are made to be found and to be sold. Profit. Aesthetic value and academic value don't show profits," Seat said callously.

"You've got to promise me something, David," Kiley said, turning sideways in the back seat of the helicopter.

"What's that?"

"I've always warned you about Frost and Sir Philip, haven't I?" she said.

"Yes, you have. And I believe it has been good for the both of us," Seat replied.

"Then I want you to assure me that nothing will happen to my sister," Kiley said.

"Kim will be safe with me," Seat said.

"Not just you, but with Sir Philip, as well," Kiley said.

"I'll do my best to protect you both. But remember, there is no honor among thieves," Seat said and then looked out the window at the sunset.

The *Calakmul Queen* had been cruising up and down the ridge for hours.

"How many sonar readings have we taken?" Jack asked.

"That's seventeen," Natalie replied.

"Correct, seventeen," Mavis confirmed. "I can't believe all the sophisticated equipment that Frost has on board. Must have cost millions."

"I bet it did," Jack replied. "Especially this device that can detect water currents up to one hundred feet deep."

"Wait," Natalie said. "There was a small surge in pressure as we came across the ridge just then."

Jack moved over and looked at the scope, which was green with yellow lines and dots.

"You're right. It was just for a fraction of a second," he said and picked up the microphone to the bridge.

"Sergeant Major, I know you must be getting tired but we need to make another run across that ridge at exactly the spot we just crossed," Jack said.

"Hold on. I'm marking the coordinates on the satellite downlink. And I'm not tired a bit. When we make a turn, I power nap for ten minutes and let Miss Heather drive her down the ridge," Kiddie said and smiled.

"Good thinking," Jack replied, as he raised his eyebrows.

"O.K., five minutes on the turn and back down to that location in one minute, twelve seconds," Kiddie replied.

"Got it," Jack replied and marked the big chart in front him. "Both of you guys watch for the mark."

"I'll help too. I'm sure they're about to go blind from the glare of all this equipment," Kim said.

As the *Calakmul Queen* neared the ridge, the three girls were ready and waiting. Jack was ready to mark the spot more accurately and Heather held her hands to the wheel like a seasoned sailor.

"Five, four, three, two, one . . . ." Jack said.

"I've got it," Natalie yelled first.

"That was it," Mavis said.

"Sergeant Major, turn around and drop anchor; we're going for a dive," Jack said.

Deep inside the blood cave of the Mayan kings, millionaire financier and artifact collector Ron Frost was draping his body with jaguar skins. He leaned over and picked up the royal, golden crown and set it on his head. One of his men had been threading quetzal feathers through it for the past hour. The green and gold of the crown was magnificent as he lay against the skin of the jaguars.

"Bring them to me and hold them up," Mr. Frost said.

Two of his men picked up the teens and propped them up next to him.

Mr. Frost leaned over and opened a brown gallon jug. When he began pouring the liquid from it over the heads of the teens, it was obvious that it was beautiful Maya Blue. He began to chant as the liquid slowly ran over their hair, over their eyelids, in their ears, and over their shoulders. Soon, every inch of their bodies was covered with the royal paint that was used to mark holy sacrifices to the gods.

Mr. Frost knew that the Mayans believed that it was the royal blue mixed with the red blood of the sacrifice that fed the rich appetite of the gods. He put down the empty jug, took a cloth from his waist, and wiped the eyes of the teens so he could see their frantic looks of horror.

"That's better. Zak Kuk will want to see your eyes when you meet her," Mr. Frost said.

"Put them across the stone," he directed his men.

The two teens were laid on their backs across the stone, which was stained black from centuries of sacrifices.

"Perfect fit," Mr. Frost said sadistically. "Bring me my knife."

One of his men brought him a genuine sacrificial knife that he had found at the new, uncharted temple northwest of Lubaantun.

"Ryan, Katelynn. There is nothing to fear. You will feel no pain. I will give you a drug that will calm you and make you relax. When you open your eyes, you will be standing before Zak Kuk, the greatest queen of all the Mayan world. She is gentle, loving, caring, and she will embrace you as your mother."

Katelynn began to sob and struggled to breath. Mr. Frost reached down and ripped the tape from her mouth, causing her lips to bleed. She took a deep breath and then shouted out to him.

"I already have a mother, you insane monster!"

Ryan tried to roll over and kick at Mr. Frost but instead rolled off the stone.

"Boss, I just got the report on my phone. The eclipse is at 3:33," the big guy said.

"Good. We'll be ahead of the schedule by five days. We've got a few hours before the ceremony. That should give you enough time to get the treasure crated and ready to move out," Mr. Frost said. "I'm going to meditate. Be sure the flotation devices are secure. We have to move the crates through the water about 1,500 feet and then up to the surface."

"So who's going to pick us up?" the man asked.

"No worries, we'll all be safe," Mr. Frost said and walked away.

Dr. Lamb's tracker led the way as Chris and Mickey followed right behind. More than once, Mickey was thankful he had selected boots instead of sandals. The light from their flashlights bounced off the bright colors of the rainforest, creating a living-tunnel effect of leaves and branches. The animals of the forest could be heard at every turn of the ancient path.

"This is the way to the oldest temple in the region that hasn't been rediscovered," Lamb said. "Archaeologists visited it about a century ago but somehow it got left out of the report, so others never became aware of it. The trees are so overgrown, it's difficult to spot from fifteen feet away."

"So what's your story, doc?" Mickey said, his detective side showing through. He was breathing easier because they were now going downhill, back toward the beach.

"I came here twenty years ago with a medical missions team. Liked it so much I kept coming back. My kids are grown; my wife Donna comes down here and works as a nurse and surgical assistant to me. She's in the next village tonight with a young woman who is having twins any day now. Then we go back home for six months. It's getting harder and harder to readjust to the city after living with these people. Their only stress is finding food and avoiding disease," Lamb said.

"I understand. I tried retirement for three months. It didn't like me very much," Mickey replied as they marched through the jungle, ducking under or grabbing branches as they went.

"Stop," Lamb said.

He turned to talk to his tracker in the local dialect for a minute.

"He says that the temple is two hundred feet ahead of us. We're to go there and he will come back for us tomorrow after the ceremony," Lamb said.

"What ceremony?" Chris asked.

"There's a total eclipse at 3:33 tomorrow afternoon. All the Maya are very wary of such events and won't go out from their homes, because they are scared of ancient pagan ceremonies. This one is especially worrisome because it is the last one before the 2012 eclipse of the Long Count," Lamb said.

"What's important about that one?" Chris asked.

"That's the day the Maya believe the earth comes to an end," Lamb said soberly.

"I see," Chris said.

"O.K., say goodbye to the guide and let's move on," Mickey said.

"What are you reading right now?" Mavis asked Jack as he scanned the scope.

"We're at high tide and the water is rushing across the ridge at one speed, but then decreases suddenly on the other side. If anything, it should pick up speed," he replied.

"Then there must be a cave down there," Ross Kiddie said as he walked up, with Heather at his side.

"I'm starved," Heather said.

"There's tons of food in the galley. Go help yourself, sweetie," Mavis replied.

"I'll go with you," Natalie said as they walked away.

"The Mayans were known to use old caves that ran under reefs and sometimes even up to the beach to connect to the cenotes," Kiddie said.

"Then if our coordinates are correct, there is a cave down

there that goes ashore, and that's where Frost is holding our kids," Jack said.

"Let's gear up and go check it," Mavis said.

"Not right now. There's millions of gallons of water rushing through that opening and down into the cave, like a long tube leading ashore. It would be too dangerous, but it matches perfectly with the point that juts out into the ocean. More than likely, the only complete underwater section is right here on the ridge," Jack said.

"We can thank Trader Jim for this clue," Mavis told Kiddie.

"Who's Trader Jim?" Kiddie asked.

"A friend in Alaska," Mavis said.

"I won't ask how a clue from someone in Alaska helped us in the Caribbean," Kiddie said and took a sip from his cup of coffee. "We're steady anchor, so I'm going to find a luxurious bed on this boat and get some sleep. I may have to do some flying at daybreak. The *Raptor* is all tied down tight in case a wind comes up during the night."

Kiddie walked out of the lounge.

"You better try to get some sleep, too," Jack said.

"But what about the radio?" Mavis said.

Kim answered, "I'll listen for it. I've been snoozing off and on while y'all were trying to figure out the ridge thing. I'm wide awake," she said and yawned.

"No, you better go get some rest. We may need you to read the hieroglyphs," Mavis said.

"I'm gone," Kim said and disappeared.

"O.K., it's just you and me until Natalie and Heather get back. Thirty minute naps. Deal?" Jack said and looked at the clock. It was nearly midnight.

Mavis lay down on the plush leather sofa and immediately fell asleep. Despite her motherly love and concern for R.O., her body couldn't take the stress any longer. Jack poured another cup of coffee and waited for the girls to come back. When they arrived they gave him a hot hamburger with pickles and ketchup.

"Where'd you get this?" he asked, surprised.

"Dad, that kitchen's got everything in the world in it," Heather said.

"And fixed just the way I like it. I feel guilty eating this knowing that Chris and Mickey are out in the jungle and your brother is, well, I can't say it," Jack said and put the hamburger down.

Natalie walked over and picked it up and held it up to his face.

"Jack, eat this so you can go save Ryan tomorrow," she said, nearly causing herself to cry. A tear escaped her left eye.

"I know. I will. Thank you," he said and took a bite.

17

Temple of the Jaguar King

"There's no moon, and even if there were, it wouldn't help much," Mickey said as he, Dr. Lamb, and Chris inched closer to the hidden temple.

"You said it was called the Temple of the Jaguar?" Chris asked Dr. Lamb.

"Yes, there are all kinds of references in the hieroglyphs about the Jaguar God and the Jaguar King: just quite a variety of information," Lamb replied.

"How did you come to know this, doc?" Mickey asked.

"Well, after twenty years of coming down here from the states, I picked up a few books and did some reading. So when I started to find a consistent pattern on this old temple, I did some inquiring about it," Lamb said.

"So you're saying that you've known about this temple for a long time and never told anyone about it," Mickey said.

"Yes. The guide brought me here several times, and to other temples over the years. But I didn't tell others about it. I didn't want the lives of these people ruined the way that tourism has impacted other villages. Sometimes it's good and people have an improvement in their standard of living.

But sometimes it's bad and modern conveniences become modern evils that cause people to change their value system. These are good people and until they want to change on their own, I'll just treat them as they are," Lamb said.

"I understand," Mickey replied. "Time to cut the lights for a bit. We need to get our cat eyes going."

They walked up to a large stone that was six feet long, four feet wide, and flat on top. It was obviously from the temple mound.

"Where are you from?" Chris asked Dr. Lamb, making small talk to deflect thoughts about R.O. and Katelynn he didn't want to consider.

"Oklahoma City," Lamb replied. "Grew up in Dallas, went to college in Lubbock at Texas Tech, settled in Oklahoma with the Air Force and just stayed there."

"My girlfriend, Natalie, is from Stillwater. She's a student at Oklahoma State. My family lives on a ranch north of Dallas," Chris said, talking into the dark void now surrounding the trio.

"Well, I guess since I'm from Amarillo, we're just a bunch of cowboys down here to show these criminals they can't mess with Texas," Mickey laughed.

"I agree with that," Lamb said.

"I haven't seen any light, so let's get moving," Mickey said.

The daring trio left the ancient rock pathway, walked across the front of the overgrown temple, and shined their lights up toward the small house built on top.

"We go about two-thirds of the way to the top and to our right we'll find a passageway that leads inside the temple to the inside layer. This temple is built on top of another temple that was built here in the seventh century," Lamb said.

"Doc, I got a feeling you know more about this temple than you're letting on," Mickey said.

"I've been here many times. I know there is an inner chamber and some crawlways that lead to who knows where. I've had a suspicion there was an inner burial chamber for years, but I felt that it would bring all kinds of chaos to the native villages if I let the truth out to the archaeological world. There hasn't been any looting, so I felt we were safe for a while longer," he said.

"Well, that's all gone now if this is Frost's location," Chris replied. "In two days, the whole world may know, one way or the other."

"Let's go," Lamb said and started to climb the eighteen-inch steps.

"Oh boy, this is going to be fun," Mickey said and started to climb.

One hour later, they had climbed over tree roots, limbs, and centuries of debris to reach the mid-level opening.

"The opening is behind this stack of wood. I put it there to be sure aerial photography wouldn't spot the opening if they got lucky and picked the temple out of the forest. With infrared, stone and rock send back different signals," Lamb said and picked up a chunk of wood and put it to the side.

Another hour passed before the opening was passable.

"It's about 2 a.m. We've got just more than twelve hours," Chris said sounding anxious.

"Let's take it slow so we don't make any mistakes," Mickey said. "How far in before we start looking for the way down, doc?"

"About fifty feet, but I'll lead the way so we can find it," Lamb said.

"No, doc, this is where you turn back. You're too valuable to those people back there and the folks we're going after are ruthless murderers," Mickey said.

"What about Chris?" Lamb said.

"From what I've learned from his family, this young man is nothing short of commando status. He's faced some pretty mean characters," Mickey replied.

"You're right. I am the odd man out. I'll be back at daylight with any help I can get," Lamb said. "Good luck." He shook hands with Mickey and Chris and started back down the ancient pyramid.

Before long Dr. Lamb's light faded away and Mickey and Chris knew it was time to face the inevitable.

"Banister to the *Queen,*" Mickey said.

"Banister to the *Queen,*" Mickey said again when he got to reply.

"This is Mavis. Just dosed off a second," she said in a hurry.

"We're going to enter a ruins area called the Temple of the Jaguar. We met a doctor from the States who thinks this might lead us to the cache location of the treasure of the kings," Mickey said, "where we hope to find the kids."

"Great. We found the tunnel to the underwater cave. We're going in at daybreak," Mavis said. "The Belizean authorities radioed that they had an emergency out at the barrier reef and couldn't be here for another day."

"Sounds typical," Mickey said. "Here's Chris."

"Mom, tell dad to be careful about the expulsion current. Watch the surge pattern. There's going to be a surge every three or four waves and the big one can throw you into a wall opening," Chris said

"I will honey. You be careful, too," she said and clicked the mike handle off.

"O.K. pardner, let's go down," Mickey said.

"I'm right behind you," Chris said as he checked the clip on the .45. It was full.

The small steps made for an awkward descent into the depths of the temple for the two Americans with size eleven shoes.

"Short people, small feet," Mickey said.

"Yes, I had to turn sideways to do this a couple of days ago," Chris replied.

"So you like this kind of stuff, I see," Mickey replied.

"No, we just got between a mad mother jaguar and some looters and had to pick an exit," Chris said.

"How'd it turn out?" Mickey asked between breaths.

"We picked an elevator that went down just a little too fast," Chris said.

"Hold it. I see some light," Mickey whispered, as he turned off his flashlight.

Chris did the same.

"Let's continue in the dark for a few minutes to be sure it wasn't my old eyes playing tricks on me," Mickey whispered.

The two took it slow, clinging to small hand and footholds as they descended deeper into the tomb.

"It's getting cool in here," Mickey said.

"We're below the floor of the forest," Chris replied.

"Sounds good to me. There's that light again," Mickey said quietly. "And I just touched down on solid rock floor."

"Me too," Chris whispered back.

The two moved closer and closer toward the source of the light, until they were looking through a small rock window about eight inches square. Below, they saw Frost's men, busily packing up stacks of gold jewelry, plates, and body armament.

"This is it," Chris said excitedly. "But how do we get down there?"

"Look over to the far wall," Mickey said and put his hand across Chris's mouth.

"R.O." Chris tried to say. "Thanks, I might have blurted it out," he whispered after Mickey took his hand away.

"Exactly. The girl is right next to them. Looks like they are sleeping, not dead," Mickey said trying to be sure that Chris stayed calm. "But they're covered in blue paint."

"Let's try to find our way down," Chris said.

"After you," Mickey said. "It's two hours until daybreak."

The two men searched the small passageway up and down and ran into one closed hall after another. Each time, they worked their way back to the small window.

"I think this king put this here just to tease his family as to how much money he had and they didn't," Mickey said on the third return to the window.

"It's now daybreak outside. Dad will be trying to find the cave entrance," Chris said and looked down at R.O. who was beginning to stir.

"Dad, Dad, wake up," Heather said as Jack opened his eyes.

She reached out and pushed his shoulders back as he instinctively started to raise up quickly.

"Mom warned me to do this lest I get a broken nose. Did she get one once?" Heather asked and smiled.

"Yes she did. Nice move," Jack replied and got up slowly.

Mavis was bringing a fresh pot of coffee from the galley. Natalie was eating the sausage and eggs that Sergeant Major Kiddie had fixed for everyone. The pain in Jack's heart returned when he remembered where they all were.

"Good morning, love. It's low tide outside. Sergeant Major Kiddie said we better get going," Mavis said. "It's nearly noon. That gives us three hours to surprise Frost."

"You're not going," Jack said.

She spun on her heels, nearly spilling the coffee.

"What are you saying?" she said.

"It's going to be me and Natalie. She's a much better diver than you are. Younger, stronger. Your hand still hasn't completely strengthened to normal since we left Hong Kong. It would be safer in case I needed a back-up diver," Jack said and walked over to her.

Mavis paused and sighed heavily.

"You're always right when it comes to matters like this. It's Natalie then," Mavis said.

"What am I doing?" Natalie said as she entered the lounge.

One hour later, everyone was on the marina deck as Jack and Natalie suited up for the dive. Sergeant Major Kiddie had fashioned an underwater sled from the frame around the remaining wave runner and attached two more tanks full of air, each with its own independent regulator. Jack and Natalie wore two each and put on Frost's ultra-expensive radio masks.

"These are better than yours are," Natalie said and tightened the strap.

"Testing, can you hear me?" Jack said with his back to Natalie.

"Yes. You're coming in clear," she said.

"The sled has neutral buoyancy, so pull it close to you so the lines don't get tangled up. Used to do this for the divers I flew out to the barrier reef," Kiddie said.

"Thank you, sir," Natalie said.

"Hey, I'm not an officer. Don't sir me," Kiddie said and smiled.

"Got a surprise for the two of you," he said and walked across the deck, where he pulled a towel off a sea scooter.

"You're a life saver," Jack said. "That should pull us through the tunnel and help us save energy to fight the tide if we need to.

"Ditto that," Natalie replied.

"Off you go," Kiddie said as he picked up the scooter and brought it over to the dive well.

Mavis kissed Jack without saying a word.

Natalie jumped into the dive well first and dropped twenty feet to the bottom of the ocean, clearing the keel of the *Queen* by eight feet. Jack was next. Then Kiddie lowered the sled with the extra tanks, followed by the sea scooter.

Jack positioned himself behind the scooter. Natalie held on to the tank sled and grabbed Jack's utility belt.

"I'm ready," she said.

"Then let's go," Jack said and switched on the scooter.

He pointed the scooter toward the ridge fifty feet ahead. They cleared the top of it, coming within fifteen feet of the surface of the ocean. Once across the top, Jack turned to his right looking for the entrance of the tunnel that had showed up on the sonar.

"There it is," Natalie said.

Jack kept the scooter at a steady speed of four miles per hour and lined up with the gaping ten-foot entrance to the cave. The closer they got, the more nervous they felt. Within seconds they were through the opening and inside the rock tube. The water was calm and fish were scurrying out of their way.

The bright light of the scooter shown far enough ahead that Jack could dodge any sudden overhangs or boulders on the cave floor.

"Are you O.K.?" Jack asked Natalie.

"I'm fine. The sled follows us like a boat trailer," she replied.

"I'll warn you if I see a floor obstruction and we have to go over the top of it," Jack said.

"O.K. I never knew how beautiful a place like this could be. There are sea fans and fish everywhere," Natalie said.

"Watch out," Jack shouted as the front of the scooter grazed the side of a six-foot reef shark headed the opposite direction, toward the opening of the tube.

"Glad we missed him," Natalie said as she watched him exit.

Soon the opening to the outside world began to fade and they both knew that if something terrible happened, there would be no one coming to save them.

18

Eclipse

Kiley Spencer and banker David Seat continued flying at tree-top level across the great expanse of the rain forest. They were sure that Frost had penetrated the hidden labyrinth that held the lost treasure of the Mayan kings.

"Patience is all we need. We've spotted some heavy equipment in the forest and his ship is anchored just off the beach. All we need is patience to intercept the cargo as he leaves. There's only one road out of the area and it takes hours to get from the coastal road down to the villages near the beach," Seat said confidently.

"But do we have someone to cover his boat?" Kiley said. She was frustrated not to be on the ground to welcome the treasure into its third millennium.

"I have contractors for just such encounters," Seat said.

"Pirates? You hired pirates?" Kiley said with her mouth open.

"One uses resources from wherever one finds them," Seat replied.

"Remind me never to cross you," Kiley said.

Deep in the Temple of the Jaguar King, Mickey and Chris had tried every possible avenue of reaching the caverns beneath it to rescue R.O. and Katelynn. Chris had even worked his way back to the outside of the temple to look for movement in the rainforest below.

"All I saw was some heavy equipment a hundred yards from the base that seemed ready to begin a big digging effort," Chris told Mickey when he returned.

"Frost is going to come down from the forest floor through all the rock and debris and extract the treasure," Mickey said. "He apparently hasn't found the cave entrance to the sea."

"But why are they attaching flotation devices to all of the inflatable containers they are filling?" Chris said. "My bet is that he is going out to sea and is going to leave all of his men hanging."

"He may be thinking about flooding the cavern and floating them upward. There's water seeping everywhere we turn down here. There's probably an underground stream coming down from the mountains. It would take days and weeks to hand-carry all that loot out of here," Mickey replied.

"Both ways don't leave much chance of survival for Ryan and Katelynn," Chris replied.

"It's 2:33. We've got sixty minutes to figure this out," Mickey said.

"Duck your head. There's an overhang ahead. Get ready, now," Jack said as he had for the past thirty minutes. "The sea scooter's battery is down to half. I hope we're getting close."

"Me too," Natalie said as she looked at her dive watch. It read 2:34. She began to worry even more.

Frost walked around the cavern anxiously and checked each and every inflatable container that his men had assembled. They had painstakingly brought down pressurized cylinders from the trucks above through the tiny opening in the forest floor and through the submerged opening to the cavern. Frost knew that the quickest way out of the cavern was through the ocean tunnel. But he had convinced his men that his trucks and crane were strong enough to penetrate the solid rock over their heads. He smiled to himself when he realized they were actually dumber than he had thought. The only item he needed from above was his environmental chamber. He had another one staged in Belize City in a warehouse. He was betting he could get there within forty-eight hours.

He looked at his watch and knew that he was just thirty minutes away from entering a new life on earth. As the reincarnated king of the Mayans, he would rule for the next thousand years. A drop of blood appeared on the face of his watch. He reached up to his forehead and felt his cracked skin. He quickly pulled up his sleeves and saw that the cracks on the surface of his arms had been growing and fluid was beginning to ooze out. Frost took out a handkerchief and wrapped it around his forehead. More blood appeared, seeping through his shirt.

He began to panic. How much time did he have? He ran through the cavern and climbed up to the floor of the jungle. He stepped into his environmental chamber and flipped the emergency cool down switch. His door shut and a vacuum was created. He looked at his watch. It was 2:50. Just thirty minutes would help, he was sure of it. Then, after the ceremony, he wouldn't need the environmental chamber. He was sure of that, too. The body of Zak Kuk would be brand new and he would be free of his disease. He sat quietly as the temperature reached 45 degrees and Schubert began to play.

He took a deep breath of the cool air and relaxed. The bleeding stopped.

Mickey and Chris watched as two men picked up R.O. and Katelynn and began to drape jaguar skins over their painted bodies. Neither had any tears left, and they simply looked at each other and tried to smile with the tape on their mouths.

They were then laid down side-by-side on the stone of sacrifice and they managed to touch one hand of the other. R.O. would mumble to get Katelynn's attention and then wink at her. He hoped that somehow his family was coming after them.

Mickey checked his watch. It was now 3:20.

"O.K., now listen," Mickey said and took a small white ball out of his pocket and turned to Chris. "I've got eight ounces of Semtex right here, and one blasting cap. I took it from the bomb on the boat. We aren't going to make it unless we go through that wall over there. I'm going to place the explosive just under the window. I want you to shoot the blasting cap. Can you do it?" Mickey said.

"Yes. I can do it," Chris replied.

"You shoot right or left?" Mickey said quickly.

"Left," Chris replied.

"Then I'm going to lean my right ear into your chest hard and cover your ears with my hands. You cover my left ear with your right hand and make the shot. If we don't do that, we might die of a concussion, wipe out all of our hearing, and not be able to save those kids," Mickey said. "Got it?"

"I got it," Chris said as he took out the Colt .45 and took it off safety.

"Here, use my CZ 75 9mm. It's got a softer squeeze. Better chance you'll hit it dead on. If you miss just a milimeter then the cap won't explode, but it will be too damaged for a second try," Mickey said and handed him the precision-made Czech handgun.

"Thanks for the added pressure," Chris said wryly. "Look, there's Frost. He's about to begin."

"O.K., let's do it," Mickey said and put his flashlight on the floor, pointing toward the explosive. He then leaned into Chris, reached up and covered Chris's ears, and pressed hard. Chris looked down and found Mickey's left ear and pressed it toward his chest with his right hand.

Raising his left hand, he took aim and began to squeeze the trigger on the CZ 75.

"Cavern straight ahead. I can see the water surface reflecting a bunch of lights. I think we've found it," Jack said to Natalie and flipped the "off" switch on the sea scooter headlight and motor and let it glide to the bottom of the cave tube.

"What do we do now?" Natalie said.

"I was hoping that by now we would have a miracle or something," Jack said.

Suddenly, a massive explosion ripped through the cavern. Small rocks flew everywhere.

Chris let go of Mickey and both were on their feet instantly, only slightly rocked by the explosion. They had been shielded by the chamber, which was chiseled out of bedrock.

R.O. opened his eyes when he heard the blast only to see Frost standing over him with the obsidian knife pulled back, ready to come down on his chest and cut out his heart. Frost, having finished a quick session in his environmental chamber, had quickly rushed down into the cave and had thrown on the King's headdress and a gold breastplate of armor. He had grabbed the ceremonial dagger just as the explosion echoed through the cave. Nothing was going to stop his insane plot now!

Mickey Banister took two steps from the hole in the wall and sent three rounds of the Colt .45 toward Frost. The first one caught him in the shoulder while the other two careened off the solid gold breastplate he wore. Frost dropped the knife, just missing Katelynn's neck. He turned and fled through the cavern.

Chris kneeled to take a shot but was driven back into the hole by a hail of gunfire from two of Frost's thugs. Mickey ran to his right, dropped into the water up to his chest, and leaned behind a boulder as several more bullets ricocheted across the cavern. He was startled when Jack and Natalie came up behind him and tapped on his leg.

He swirled around and put the gun right between Jack's eyes.

"Sorry. Glad you made it. Chris is pinned down over by the big hole in the wall. The kids are twenty-five yards that way, still on their backs. Frost took off into the other cavern," Mickey shouted over the noise of rapid fire pistols.

"We've got enough gear to get us back out of here," Jack said and produced a Glock .40 caliber pistol from beneath his wet suit. "These fire underwater, don't they?"

"Sure do. That's what the Sergeant Major said when he gave me one, too," Natalie said with a smile.

"O.K., on three Jack and I are going to lay down fire, and you take a run to get the kids untied," Mickey said to Natalie.

She quickly unfastened her tanks and rose to one knee next to Mickey. With the .45 in one hand and the Glock in the other Mickey counted to three. He and Jack rose up from the boulder and started firing. Natalie ran as fast as she could and slid to a halt behind the sacrificing stone. She reached up to rip the tape off their mouths first to be sure they could breath.

"Oh, my gosh," Katelynn started.

"Shhh, we've got to get up and run to the water," Natalie said as she took the obsidian knife and cut their hands and feet free. Two rounds ricocheted off the cave wall behind them and they all three ducked.

"O.K., run and jump in the water," Natalie yelled as they all took off in a sprint.

Just as they reached the water's edge a bullet ripped through Natalie's wet suit and broke the zipper behind her neck.

"Ow," she screamed as she hit the water next to Jack, reaching for the back of her neck.

Jack's gun went empty. Natalie turned in the water, and he saw the blood on her neck. He pulled her up close to him and put his hand over the wound.

"Just broke the skin," Jack said and he could see the relief on her face. "Tell R.O. to take Katelynn down to the sled and put the regulator in her mouth. Tell her not to panic, this may be her first time to dive," Jack said. "There's a spare mask on the front of the scooter."

Natalie started to leave, then turned back.

"Where's Chris?" she said with a worried look on her face.

"He's still in the temple. He's pinned down but we're going to get him out. Now go," Jack said.

Natalie hooked on her gear and swam over to R.O. and told him the plan. Katelynn nodded her head in agreement the whole time. Soon all three were on the bottom of the cave tube, putting on the spare equipment that the Sergeant Major had thought to send along.

Chris looked out across the cavern at the boxes and boxes of packed treasure. He checked his clip. He had two rounds left when he noticed the satchel that Mickey was carrying was lying on the ground next to him. He opened it and dumped out three water bottles, a round of salami, and two spare clips for the CZ 75. He grinned from ear to ear. He also found another ball of Semtex, smaller than the first.

He looked out to where Jack and Mickey were pinned and could see that R.O. and Katelynn were no longer on the sacrificial stone. He thought for a minute and then took one of the 9 mm rounds from the spare clip and pressed it into the small ball of Semtex. He knew that he would have only one more try. Locating the best position, he ran toward the opening and threw the bomb material as hard as he could toward a wall next to Frost's men, who were still firing.

When he slid behind the wall, Chris leaned forward to take his shot but couldn't find the explosive. He looked around and then raced back across the opening. He then looked toward Mickey and motioned to him with a throwing arm, hoping he would understand.

"I got cha, young feller," Mickey said, and nodded his understanding to Chris.

"What's happening?" Jack said.

"Looks like you got a bright son there, but he needs to work on his pitching arm," Mickey said.

He leaned forward against the boulder and took off his now-ruined Panama hat. Focusing with his dominant right eye and gripping the Colt .45 with both hands, he took aim at the small ball of Semtex with the back end of the 9 mm round pointed right at him.

"Here's one for Ryan and Katelynn," Mickey said and squeezed off a round.

Before he could blink, the explosion ripped through the cavern and killed Frost's men. Water began rushing from the side of the wall. Chris pushed the CZ under his belt, ran with all his might toward the pool of water, and dove in head first, landing a few feet from Natalie.

"O.K. Special Agent, it's your turn to swim," Jack said and put the regulator in Mickey's mouth and pushed him under.

In less than two minutes, Natalie was pulling the sled with the sea scooter. She knew they only had ten minutes of juice left. R.O. and Katelynn were hanging on with plenty of air. Jack had shoved his octopus spare regulator in Mickey's mouth, who was busy holding his nose with his eyes closed.

Natalie had reached out and pulled Chris up close to her, and she had given him her spare regulator. The sudden surge of fresh water from the side of the cave created a current that was sending them all down the tube, gaining speed.

"Hang on," Jack yelled to Natalie who signaled the others.

In a matter of minutes, the beleaguered heroes and their two rescued teens were bobbing in the warm Caribbean. The daylight was still hazy, because the sun was just beginning to appear from behind the moon. The eclipse was over and the sun became bigger and brighter and brighter.

"Did you see that?" Natalie said to Chris.

"Yes, almost too close," he replied and kissed her. "Now you're my hero," he said and kissed her again.

"Oh gosh, someone nearly cuts my heart out and look what I wake up to see," R.O. said, bobbing in the water from a few feet away.

"I think it's romantic," Katelynn said, pulling the hair out of her face.

"You do?" R.O. said.

Epilogue

"Dear Drew"

As the eclipse left the sky, two black zodiacs skimmed across the water's surface at high speed. Aboard each zodiac were three men, dressed in black wetsuits and carrying automatic machine guns. As they zoomed by the *Calakmul Queen,* Heather almost fell off the wave runner she was driving out to help the stranded heroes. The first zodiac reached Jack and Mickey.

"Dr. MacGregor?" one of the men asked.

"Yes, I'm MacGregor," Jack replied.

"We're United States Navy Seals dispatched to assure your safety. We got here as soon as we could. Have your children been reacquired?" the younger man asked quickly.

"Yes, they're here with us in the water. We're not sure if the kidnappers might be right behind us in the water or at the tree line," Jack said.

"That's a roger," the seal barked some orders into his radio. Within seconds, two black helicopters appeared from across Wild Cane Cay and headed for the beach.

"Let's get you on board and to your boat," the Seal said as he reached for Mickey.

"Mickey Banister, FBI," he said as he was pulled into the zodiac.

"Good to meet you, sir. We were alerted of your presence and to acquire you as well," the young man said.

"Well I guess they didn't want me in retirement after all," Mickey said and helped R.O. and Katelynn climb aboard.

Suddenly they heard gunfire from the tree line where the Seals had landed and run ashore. It was over as quickly as it had started. The Seal in the zodiac received a radio message and turned to Mickey.

"Special Agent Banister, the threat has been reduced to zero," he said. "And Captain Morton sends his regards."

"David Morton! Tell him thank you. Where is he?" Jack responded, crawling into the rubber boat.

"He's the skipper on the recovery ship just over the horizon," the Seal replied.

"Thanks guys," Jack said as the Seals helped him aboard the *Calakmul Queen* and then turned the zodiac to head out to sea across the gentle Caribbean.

The MacGregors and friends watched as the Seals boarded the two black helicopters and soon disappeared on the other side of the island. Within a few minutes, everyone was being loaded onto the *Calakmul Queen* and they were receiving hugs and kisses from Mavis and Kim. The two boats full of Seals saluted Sergeant Major Kiddie when they learned his rank and turned the zodiacs back out to sea where they would be picked up by a support boat or helicopter; no one would ever know which, and neither would the country of Belize.

"They know better than to salute me," Kiddie said from the marina deck watching the rubber boats disappear in the distance.

"It's called respect," Mickey said and toweled off more.

"I know and I do appreciate it. Respect is hard to get any more for what I used to do," Kiddie said.

"That makes two of us," Mickey added.

Heather came running down the stairs.

"Y'all need to come topside and take a look at this," Heather nearly shouted.

When the tired and beleaguered crew reached the deck outside the lounge and turned toward the shore, they could now see dozens of floating crates.

"Oh my goodness. Is that what I think it is?" Kim said.

"It's the treasure," Chris said. "The water rushing from the spring in the side of the cave must have been enough to fill the cavern with water and push all the crates down the tube and out to sea."

"Anyone have enough strength to go get them?" Jack asked.

"I'm ready," Kim Spencer said and they all laughed.

Over the next few hours until the sun set over the Maya Mountains, the *Calakmul Queen* became the new home of the lost treasure of the Mayan Kings.

Each room in the yacht was bursting with gold and artifacts that would fill many museums and add to the wealth of knowledge of the ancient culture.

"Jack, who was that you were talking to on the beach?" Mavis asked.

"That was Dr. Robert Lamb. He discovered the Temple of the Jaguar . . ."

"For which he will be given credit," Kim interrupted.

"And he wanted to let me know that his tracker had found the body of a man who had cracked skin and had bled to death from cuts all over his body," Jack said. "He said he looked like he had been attacked by a jaguar."

"Frost?" Mavis said.

"Yes, he had identification on him, as well. It was definitely Frost," Jack replied.

"So it was his greed that killed him," Mavis said.

"I'm glad," R.O. exclaimed with Katelynn standing next to him. "He deserved to die."

"Oh kids. What are we going to do? What happened to you was horrible," Mavis said.

"Don't worry about it, Dr. MacGregor. We're still alive

and now we're best friends forever," Katelynn said and hugged her.

"That is so sweet," Kim said as the kids walked away. "I'm just disappointed that my sister, Kiley, wasn't here to see all of this. She would have been so excited, but that's what she gets for hanging out with all those Scuba hunks at the barrier reef resorts."

Little did they know that Kiley Spencer and David Seat had made an effort to move in on the operation just as the explosion and gunfire had opened up. Not being violent, confrontational types, they circled overhead and watched the Navy Seals arrive and quickly dispatch the shore team that Frost had arranged to take all the treasure away. Knowing when to cut and run, they flew their helicopter back to Belize City to lick their wounds and talk about how much they has lost that day. They lived to steal again another day.

Mickey was fast asleep on a leather couch. Jack was opening the written message that the Navy Seal gave to him.

"Greetings from Trader Jim," it read.

"Jim, you son of a gun," Jack said and turned to tell Mavis.

Chris and Natalie were asleep in each other's arms on deck in a big hammock.

R.O. and Katelynn were sitting in Frost's office in front of a computer. R.O. had just keyed in the email address of his friend Drew Nevius, back home in Texas. His first sentence began, "Dear Drew, how's your new friend Morgan Vogel? You won't believe what happened to me today . . ."